Lured by forbidding fascination...

As I stood on the boardwalk before Raven's Rise, I knew that we were linked irrevocably, this great brooding structure and I. I wanted to walk up the steps and enter the wide entry hall, go into the library with its book-lined walls, drift silently through the maze of endless corridors—

Some whisper of sound caused me to whirl quickly around, and a scream froze in my throat as I saw the figure standing not far behind me. He was a giant of a man. The pale light from a sliver of moon caught a shine of metal, and I realized that a shotgun dangled from one huge hand....

LEGACY OF RAVEN'S RISE

HELEN B. HICKS

Harlequin Books

TORONTO • NEW YORK • LONDON
AMSTERDAM • PARIS • SYDNEY • HAMBURG
STOCKHOLM • ATHENS • TOKYO • MILAN

Published September 1985
ISBN 0-373-32008-6

Printed in Canada

CHAPTER ONE

FROM THE MOMENT I ARRIVED in Bittercreek, the house called Raven's Rise held an uneasy fascination for me. The massive structure sat atop a large knoll athwart the west end of the short main street. Its soaring turrets and rounded conical tower blocked the afternoon sun and cast a dark and brooding shadow over the town.

As I gazed at it, a chill ran through me. I was tempted to climb back into the stagecoach and continue on to some warmer, more welcoming environ. But before I could act on this foolish impulse, the driver had winnowed my shabby luggage from an assortment on the roof of his vehicle and set it on the dusty wooden sidewalk.

I turned to thank him and to my surprise saw that he was retrieving yet another suitcase, this one an expensive-looking Gladstone bag. I glanced quickly at the stagecoach. One of the passengers with whom I had shared the long, uncomfortable ride from San Francisco had emerged and was standing beside it. His eyes met mine, and he smiled, a slow, amused smile that lit their hazel depths.

I blushed hotly and looked away. The man was so strikingly handsome that I hadn't been able to keep from staring at him during the journey. Most of the time he had been courteous enough to seem absorbed in the barren countryside through which we passed, but I knew that he had been very much aware of my obsession. If I had dreamed that his destination was the same as mine, I would have put a stronger rein on my curiosity.

Deliberately, I turned my back to him and considered the problem of my luggage. The trunk, though small, was heavier than I could manage easily. I glanced about for a porter or for some strapping youngster eager to earn a nickel by carrying it across to the hotel. But the stage's arrival was apparently not an exciting event in Bittercreek. The broad, tree-lined street stood empty under the late-afternoon sun, and the stage driver had disappeared. With dismay, I realized that I would have to manage by myself.

I picked up my carpetbag, but before I could reach for the trunk, a firm male hand closed over its leather handle.

"May I?" the handsome man asked pleasantly. "I assume we are headed in the same direction."

"Why should you assume any such thing?" I retorted more tartly than was necessary. I was still smarting from the amusement I had seen in his eyes.

"Because you are a stranger to Bittercreek and there is only one hotel in town." He picked up my trunk as though it held nothing more substantial than feathers.

I glanced about. Other than a few elegant private residences, none of which was as ornate and imposing as the mansion on the knoll, there were only three two-story buildings: the brick-fronted bank, a square stone structure with I.O.O.F. printed in large letters on its front and the hotel he had indicated, directly across the street. Several of the other businesses sported false fronts—a carryover, I supposed, from the gold-mining town this had been some twenty years ago. None seemed a haven for weary travelers.

Reluctantly, I said, "I suppose so. But mightn't I have come to visit relatives or friends?"

He smiled again, the action creating engaging crinkles at the outer corners of his eyes. I decided he was much too handsome to be trusted.

"Bittercreek is very small, as you see," he answered, graciously overlooking my truculent tone. "It is highly improbable that anyone would have a relative as lovely as you and not have made the entire town aware of it."

I felt heat burn along my cheekbones. Either his remark was sheer flattery, or he was making fun of me, for I had been taught from an early age that flaming hair and a spattering of freckles did not a beauty make. However, I do have eyes of a quite nice shade of green. Perhaps he had a penchant for that. I decided to accept his fortuitous offer of help and started toward the hotel.

He fell in beside me, each of his long strides covering two of mine. After a short while he asked plaintively, "What do you have in your trunk? Bricks? It grows heavier by the step."

"Books," I answered. I had not been able to part with a special few that my foster father had given me.

He eyed me with mock horror. "Surely you aren't the new schoolteacher! Our lads will be totally distracted from their studies."

I had been right in my suspicions; he was making sport of me. "I am not a teacher. I simply enjoy reading," I replied tersely. "I am in Bittercreek because—" I caught myself. I was not ready to tell anyone that. "Because it sounded like an interesting place," I finished lamely.

He laughed, but the hazel eyes were assessing me. "Interesting? It's a stagnant backwater, a relic of the gold-mining days that years ago should have been abandoned and left to crumble into dust. I haven't yet figured out why it wasn't. We do have our claim to fame, however. A state senator is among our wealthier residents."

I refused to appear impressed, though it did seem odd that such a person would live in this unimportant town. "Is that huge place his?" I could not help asking. I nodded toward the forbidding mansion. His glance followed mine.

"No. Until recently that was the home of the town's most fascinating citizen, Miss Raven Winfield. It is known as Raven's Rise."

As I heard the strange, exotic name for the first time, a mixture of fear and longing came over me. I gazed at the house. The setting sun had edged its irregular outline with a fiery nimbus, leaving a dark mass silhouetted against the flaming sky. I felt drawn to it and yet repelled. Eager questions trembled on my lips, but the stranger had opened the hotel door and was politely waiting.

I stepped inside. The lobby of the Bittercreek Hotel was small, neat and well kept. Clean lace curtains hung at the small-paned windows, and in a niche beside the stairs a potted plant added a cool and pleasant note. The stranger and I crossed to the waist-high mahogany counter, where he set down my trunk and bowed in a graceful gesture.

"Allow me to introduce myself," he said. "I am Marcus Hannaford. If I may be of any further service—"

"Thank you, but no." I fought to keep my tone coolly distant. It was hard to resist his pleasant demeanor and the kind and considerate way that he spoke, but he was not the only man to attempt that approach with me. I had not come all the way from San Francisco to be seduced by the first attractive male whose glance I caught. I tilted my slightly retroussé nose a little higher and reached to touch the silver bell on the desk. It rang imperiously.

As a spare, gray-haired man approached from some back room, I kept my eyes resolutely on him, ignoring Marcus Hannaford's second bow and murmured response. He picked up his bag, which he had set beside mine, and proceeded to the stairs. I sensed, rather than saw, him leave and felt both relief and a ridiculous disappointment. Apparently I had not expected him to give up quite so easily.

The desk clerk looked at me without so much as a smile of greeting.

"I would like a room," I said. Something in his expression caused me to dispense with genialities.

He took his time about answering. "You got a reservation?" he asked at last. There was no warmth in his tone.

"Why, no." I was conscious of a sudden tightening in my chest. "I didn't suppose that one would be necessary."

"We're full up." Gray eyes met mine coldly. "If you hurry, you can catch the stage before it leaves."

I recoiled a little with the shock of his rude words, then glanced at the cubbyholes behind the desk. Most of them had the keys still in them. I realized that the man was quite brazenly lying, but for what reason I could not imagine.

"Nonsense!" Marcus Hannaford said sharply. I glanced around and saw that he had come partway down the stairs again. "Harper, the hotel hasn't been filled in fifteen years! What do you mean by refusing a room to this young lady?"

I felt my cheeks grow warm. Why hadn't the man gone upstairs where he belonged, instead of reappearing to witness my humiliation? "I can handle this, thank you," I began. "There is no need—"

The clerk's words cut into mine as though I hadn't spoken. "Well, they ain't filled exactly, Marcus," he began evasively, "but some of them's closed off permanent. Ain't been dusted in a long spell."

"Well, dust one!" I demanded before Mr. Hannaford could insert his two cents' worth. "And immediately, or I shall report you to the owner."

I could see by his sour look that he was not properly squelched. "That don't cut any ice with me, missy, seeing as I'm him." He cast another glance at

Marcus and reached for a key. "But you can have this one. I expect it ain't too bad. First, though, you got to sign the book."

I was stung by his grudging tone and by the obvious fact that I owed his acceptance of me to the presence of Mr. Hannaford, but I was in no position to quibble. I swallowed my pride and took the key, then signed the register in my plain, unadorned handwriting. Selina Ames. As always, I wondered what it should really say.

I looked up. Mr. Harper was watching me sourly, and as I laid down the pen, he swung the book around and stared at my name, then, without a change of expression, came around the desk and shouldered my trunk with no more apparent difficulty than Mr. Hannaford had had.

"Come on," he said impatiently. "Room's at the top of the stairs."

He sounded as though he expected me to scurry up the stairs before him like an upbraided scullery maid, but I refused to be intimidated, and with Mr. Harper huffing and fuming just behind me, I ascended with the pace and dignity of a queen. As I unlocked the door to the room that he indicated, he pushed past me and set the trunk in the middle of the flowered carpet, then, with another baleful look, left me. His manner disturbed me. Why would I, a stranger in a strange town, be greeted with instant animosity?

I continued to ponder this as I unpacked and settled into the pleasant, scrupulously clean bed-sitting room. Could the man's hostility have something to do with the mysterious reason I had been summoned here? Not summoned, I amended, but invited. The anonymous letter had simply said that it would be to my benefit if I came to Bittercreek and that if I did so I might unlock the secret of my past. But the two hundred dollars that accompanied it I had construed as an emphatic invitation.

I took out the money and the letter from a hidden compartment of my carpetbag and thrust them deep into my pocketbook. No need to read the missive again; its creases were worn from frequent refolding. This was the first hint I had ever received that anyone on earth could enlighten me as to the mysteries of my parentage. Even now the memory of that first excitement caused my hands to tremble and my heart to beat faster.

I reached into my pocketbook again and took out the small velvet pouch I always carried; loosening it, I shook its contents into my open palm. The enormous emerald gleamed richly in its circlet of small, clear diamonds. I slipped the ring from its thin gold chain and onto my finger. It fit almost perfectly. My foster father had told me that it and the chain had been around my neck when he had rescued me from the fire; until now it had been my only link with the shrouded and unimaginable past. I touched it gently. It reminded me of him, for he had given it into my care not long before he died.

Reluctantly, I put the emerald back into its velvet nest. Much as I had always longed to wear it, I had felt it too large and ornate for someone in my situation. During these past two difficult years I had often considered selling it but somehow had never brought myself to do so. Perhaps now, I thought, brightening a little, the ring would help me to determine if there was truth to the possibilities presented by my unknown benefactor.

I glanced at the little enameled clock that I had taken from my trunk and set on the bedside stand. It was growing late. If I didn't hurry, the hotel dining room would no doubt close, and I realized suddenly that I was ravenously hungry. Quickly, I put the empty luggage in the closet and set about erasing some of the stains of my journey.

The oaken washstand at which I bathed held a huge china basin embellished with hand-painted full-blown roses. A matching pitcher filled with fresh water was mute testimony to the hotel owner's untruth about the readiness of the room. On what, I wondered again, did he base his antipathy? Was my benefactor the only person to know of my background, or did perhaps many of this small town's inhabitants know more than I did about my shadowed past? I recoiled at the idea and hastily turned my thoughts to the problem of what I might wear to dinner.

I didn't have many choices. My small salary as a ladies' companion had covered only my simplest needs and had not yielded enough to replenish my wardrobe beyond the barest necessities. However, I did have a few presentable gowns from the halcyon days when I was still treated as a daughter of the house. One of these, a pale green challis with a low neckline and a series of tucks down the insert in the front, was my favorite. Hastily, I shook it out and slipped it over my head. After brushing my hair and catching it back with a tailored bow of the same material, I patted a little rice powder over my cheeks and nose in a vain attempt to hide the freckles, bit my lips to redden them and went downstairs.

I had not admitted to myself that I was dressing for the possibility that I would encounter Mr. Hannaford, but when my quick glance about the lobby failed to find him, I felt again that ridiculous disappointment.

Neither was he in the small dining room, which adjoined the lobby by an open set of double doors. Feeling somewhat self-conscious, I went quickly to a nearby vacant table and sat down, for the two couples and several single men still dining were eyeing me with considerable curiosity.

The young woman who came to take my order was neat and wholesome looking. She smiled pleasantly as she handed me the menu and stood quietly awaiting my decision.

"The pot roast, I think," I said, handing it back to her.

"A good choice, miss. It's especially nice this evening." She went briskly toward the kitchen, and I was left to occupy myself by studying the other diners, who had returned their attention to their food.

Or so I thought at first. As my idle gaze touched one after the other, I realized that they were all surreptitiously watching me, and if I could judge by the low-toned conversations, talking about me, as well. Only one, a rather short, tired-looking man in his mid- to late fifties, had a kindly demeanor. The glances of the others were as cold and unwelcoming as had been the slate-gray stare of the elderly hotel owner.

I tried to tell myself that I was imagining it, but I knew that I was not. And I was profoundly disturbed. It couldn't be that this was simply an unfriendly town, for surely a man in the hotel business wouldn't subscribe to that attitude. I could only assume that something about me, either my manner of dress or my resemblance to someone whom these people had reason to dislike, caused their forbidding attitudes toward me.

After scarcely touching my dinner—for my hunger had completely deserted me—I paid my small bill and left the dining room. I started to go upstairs, but the pain that strictured my chest made the thought of that empty room unbearable. Instead, I went outside and stood on the porch, breathing in the warm night air and waiting for my agitation to abate somewhat. I felt perilously near to tears. I had undertaken this journey with such hope, such joy in the thought that perhaps at last I would find someone bound to me by blood, for surely that person would have to love me. And so far I had been met with mostly hostility.

Marcus Hannaford was striding purposefully toward the hotel. Quickly, I stepped off the porch and into the shadow of the towering oaks that lined the street, for I dared not meet him, feeling as I did. I would be likely to succumb to his blandishments without a struggle.

The dust of the road was velvet soft under my feet, and I made no sound as I drifted along beneath the wan light of a quarter moon. My impulsive flight had

d the dark bulk of Raven's Rise, and
I forgot my loneliness and hurt. The
completely deserted. I walked along the
gs that enclosed it until I reached the central
gate, then stood staring. I felt again a strange sensation of being drawn to it and yet repelled.

I had no idea how long I stood there, barely conscious of the warm breeze whispering against my cheek
and of the pungent smell of oak that scented the evening air. What must it be like to live in such grandeur,
I wondered, and what had happened to Miss Raven
Winfield, that fascinating woman with the exotic
name whose home it had been? Had she tired of the
sameness of life in a small town and gone to seek excitement in the city? Or had she met a tragic and untimely death, as befitted one who inhabited a place of
such somber splendor? I yearned to know more about
her, to understand her, if it were possible, as thoroughly as I understood myself.

Just then a handbreadth of cloud eclipsed the
moon. Instantly, the mansion became a huge, shape-
less mass looming over me, and I clutched the metal
bars of the gate and shivered with sudden, nameless
terror. As I stood, transfixed and scarcely breathing,
I saw that deep within the black interior of the house
a tiny firefly of light was flitting erratically about.

CHAPTER TWO

IN SPITE OF THE BALMINESS of the evening, I was shaking with chill when I reached my room at the hotel. After I had undressed and gotten into bed, I was grateful for the warmth of the quilted coverlet. Why the flickering light should have imparted to me a sense of evil, or for what reason I had felt that sudden terror of the mansion, I had no idea; only a moment before, I had been quite passionately envying the woman who had owned it. But a residual fear still held me in its grip, and it was a long time before I fell asleep.

When I awoke, full sunlight was streaming in through the open window, and the fear had gone, leaving in its wake only a faint shadow of unease. I tried to banish that, too, as I rose and began to dress.

My immediate concern, I reminded myself as I bathed in the tepid water of the china ewer, was where or how to begin my search for my true identity. I decided that I must make at least one or two friends among the townspeople. Surely, I thought, everyone in Bittercreek couldn't be prepared to dislike me. There was that pleasant young waitress and the kindly, tired-looking man in the dining room. And, of course, Marcus Hannaford.

I didn't allow myself to think about him.

I chose my morning's apparel with great deliberation. If, I reasoned, I took care to appear young and
fresh and possibly a trifle naive, people might feel
more predisposed to return my friendly overtures.
Accordingly, I chose the simplest of my dresses: a
green-and-white candy stripe whose prim starched
collar and cuffs lent it an air of innocence. After
brushing my hair, I caught it loosely at the nape with
a narrow ribbon, coaxed a few soft tendrils into place
around my face and stepped back to consider my reflection in the somewhat spotted mirror above the
bureau. To my satisfaction, I scarcely looked to be a
day over eighteen.

And then I spoiled the entire effect by wearing the
emerald ring.

I hadn't planned to, certainly. I had simply been
changing my belongings to a pocketbook that better
matched my gown and had stopped, as I nearly always did, to admire the ring. Suddenly, achingly, I
wanted to wear it, to show the world, and particularly
the people in this town, that Selina Ames was a person to be reckoned with. For I knew with a certainty
born of long observation that I would not meet with
indifference or contempt while wearing a ring such as
this, no matter how inappropriate it might appear.
Defiantly, I slipped it on my finger and went
downstairs.

In the dining room, the rosy-cheeked young woman
was again waiting tables. It had occurred to me that
while the town had no other hotel, there might be
someone who let rooms upon occasion. After she had

taken my order, I asked her if she knew of such a place.

"There's not much call for that," she said slowly, a frown creasing her high, rounded forehead. "Most folks just spend a night or two, and then they're on their way." Her expression cleared. "But ma has an extra room. It's not fancy, but it's clean. And she'd welcome the company."

Considering the girl's fastidious appearance, I thought it might be just the thing. "Please talk to her about it," I said, "and let me know if she approves."

She nodded and moved off toward the kitchen, returning immediately with a steaming cup of coffee. As I sipped it, the tired-looking man came in, gave me a friendly nod and sat down to retire behind a newspaper. Idly, I speculated about him. Could he be a banker, perhaps, or a lawyer? I doubted it. His hair and mustache were shaggy, and his clothing was somewhat worn and rather carelessly attended to.

Then my attention was drawn to his newspaper, whose title I could read from my chair.

The *Bittercreek Bulletin*.

I stared at it with rising excitement. If the town had a newspaper, if only a weekly, its office must have retained back issues. And in those issues there might possibly be a clue as to why I had been invited here.

"Where is the newspaper office?" I asked when the waitress brought my breakfast. "And has it been publishing long?"

"It's just down the street," she answered. "As for how long it's been publishing, I couldn't say. But I can find out for you." She raised her voice a trifle. "Say,

Doc, how old is the *Bulletin*?'' To me, she added, ''Doc Gentry's been here since the town began, they tell me. Came to hunt gold and stayed to dose everybody in the place at one time or another.''

I felt a slight chagrin. I should have guessed. He looked just as I might have expected a country doctor to look. The only thing lacking was a little black bag.

He glanced up from his newspaper. His eyes had not lost their kindly look. ''It's been here nearly as long as I have, Ellie. Twenty years, at least. Though the editor's new. Couldn't have been here more than five, six years at the most.'' He smiled at me. ''Why? Is the young lady fixing to start a rival sheet?''

I laughed. ''Hardly. I was just surprised that so small a place should have a newspaper. I will have to subscribe. Surely that will be a good way to get to know a town.''

''It would seem so.'' His look was suddenly intent. ''Then you plan to stay for an extended visit, Miss—?''

''I am Selina Ames, Dr. Gentry. And I am not sure what my plans are at the moment.'' Some of my previous caution returned. ''Is there any reason why I shouldn't stay?''

''Not at all. I expect you will bring this creaky old town some much-needed fire and sunshine. But please go on with your breakfast before it is entirely cold.''

He went back to his newspaper, and Ellie winked at me. ''Doctor's orders,'' she whispered with a little giggle. I proceeded to finish my meal with a good appetite.

BEFORE VISITING the newspaper office, I decided I must deposit the two hundred dollars in the bank. It was nearly all the money I had, for I had spent my own small savings on the stagecoach ticket; if I should lose it, I would be in great difficulty. Lifting my skirts carefully from the powdery dust of the street, I crossed to the square brick building.

The interior of the bank was musty-smelling and somewhat chilly, as though the morning sun had not penetrated its thick walls. It was surprisingly ornate, considering the size of the town, and had a heavy marble counter and filigreed brass grillwork. A pale young man worked with fierce concentration behind one of the two wickets, the other of which was empty. An older, portly man was sitting at a large oaken desk behind a fencelike partition. As I hesitated, he glanced up almost impatiently then quickly shut his ledger and rose.

"Yes, young lady. What can I do for you?"

"I would like to open an account."

"Certainly. Just step this way, Miss—?" He opened the little gate for me and indicated a chair.

"Ames," I answered. "Selina Ames." I read the plaque on his desk. "I am afraid it is just a small account, Mr. Soames, hardly worthy of the attention of the bank's president."

"Each of our clients is of equal importance," Mr. Soames said unctuously. After seating me, he bustled back to his large swivel chair. I was vaguely aware that the young teller had ceased his work and was watching us. "What will it be? Checking or savings?"

"Savings. In the amount of two hundred dollars."

His eyebrows rose. "That seems a rather large sum for a young lady such as yourself to be carrying."

Though his tone was fatherly, the eyes were not. It was as though they wished to probe into the secret recesses of my brain.

"It is part of an inheritance," I lied without compunction. I took out the money and laid it on the desk before him. "It might be considered a legacy from the past."

He stared, and I was suddenly conscious of the weight of the emerald ring. "I—see." His pudgy hands fumbled aimlessly with some papers on his desk. "Ames, you said. And the address?"

"At the moment I have a room at the hotel."

He picked up a pen but still didn't put it to paper. "You expect to be with us for an extended length of time?"

With a dignity I couldn't have summoned without the ring, I gave him a level look and didn't answer. When the pause became significant, he shrugged and said with a forced geniality, "Just the friendly curiosity of a small town."

I wanted to say that I had not yet seen much evidence of the friendliness he mentioned, but the door opened, and Marcus Hannaford came in. He started toward the banker, then, seeing that he was occupied, stopped just beyond the gate.

Mr. Soames glanced at him. "Heard you were back." His tone was barely cordial.

"The bad penny," Marcus said, as though in agreement with the banker's unspoken opinion. He smiled at me. "I have some business to discuss,

Soames, but I see you are more pleasantly occupied at the moment. Good morning, Miss Ames."

"You two have met?" The banker's tone held surprise and what almost sounded like dismay.

"I had the good fortune to travel from San Francisco with the young lady. It brightened an otherwise tedious journey." Marcus spoke with grave courtesy, but his eyes held laughter. "I trust you enjoyed your evening stroll, Miss Ames. The air was pleasant after the heat of the day."

So he had seen my undignified plunge from the hotel porch last night and had guessed that I was avoiding him. Embarrassment surged through me, but this time it was followed by self-disgust. Really, I berated myself, the man had done nothing to deserve such rudeness; in fact, the walk might have been much pleasanter with him as my escort, and I might have not experienced that moment of terror at the mansion's gate. I imagined him strolling beside me, his long strides shortened to accommodate mine, the handsome head bent attentively to catch my every word.

With a start of surprise I realized that both Marcus and Mr. Soames were watching me, the banker with slight bewilderment and Marcus with an amused and penetrating look that seemed to fathom my very thoughts. Rising hastily, I said, "Why, yes, I—It was—" I gathered my wits together. "Mr. Soames and I have quite finished, Mr. Hannaford. You are perfectly free to conduct your business."

Leaving him time for no more than a murmured response, I fled the building. It was not until I had reached the walk outside that I realized I had forgotten my new bankbook.

I stood, undecided. Should I go back for it and by doing so encounter the amusement in those hazel eyes again? I could not face it. Mr. Soames would no doubt send the book to the hotel; if not, I would return for it later. Quickly, I crossed the street and went in the direction of the newspaper office.

I thought at first that the office was empty, but as I approached the scarred oak counter, I saw a man sitting at a huge rolltop desk that stood against one wall. His back was toward me, and I could see only a shock of unruly black hair above thin shoulders garbed in white shirt and vest. He didn't seem to have heard me enter, and I cleared my throat somewhat ostentatiously. At once, he leapt to his feet and whirled to face me; as he did so, he plucked a coat from the back of his chair in one swift motion. He slipped it on and buttoned it neatly while coming to greet me.

"Good morning!" His geniality seemed genuine. "How may I help you?"

I was immediately taken by his appearance. Though he was not tall and was very slim, there was a whipcord look about him that spoke of hidden strength, and he had pale skin that threw his thick black brows and heavy mass of hair into startling contrast. But it was his eyes that most intrigued me. They were a deep, clear blue of startling intensity, and just now they gazed into mine as though my answer to his mundane question was of the utmost importance. It was a moment before I could think to answer.

"I would like to take out a subscription to the newspaper." I felt a little ashamed, as though my ordinary request would doom him to disappointment. But that didn't seem to be the case.

"Wonderful!" he exclaimed eagerly. "That means that Bittercreek has acquired another citizen. I am Jared Newcomb, editor of this intrepid sheet. Welcome to our little hamlet." Briskly, he pushed a pad and pencil toward me. "If you will write your name and place of residence, I'll see that the paper is delivered promptly each Thursday." He grinned. "In fact, I'll deliver it myself. The *Bittercreek Bulletin* is strictly a one-man operation."

"I see." His humor was infectious, and as I picked up the pen, I found myself returning his smile. "The name is Selina Ames." I wrote it on the tablet. "As to the address—" I paused in some confusion. "I think I will be staying at the home of Ellie, the waitress in the hotel dining room." I hesitated, then confessed, "I don't even know her last name."

"Ah, but I do." He pulled the notepad to him and with bold, heavy strokes followed my name with a short address. "Henderson," he said, without looking up. "And you'd be wise to take your meals there. Ellie's ma bakes biscuits that have to be tied to the table so they won't float away before they can be eaten."

I laughed, and for the first time since arriving in Bittercreek, felt genuinely at ease. "I'll remember," I said. Then my smile faded as I recalled my real reason for being there. "There is one thing more. Would it be possible for me to look through the back issues of your newspaper? I thought that might help me decide whether or not I should settle here.''

For a moment I was afraid that I had volunteered too much, for something close to skepticism touched the lean features. But the look was gone so quickly I might have imagined it. ''Certainly you may see them,'' he replied. ''Do you plan to start at the beginning of the town's history, or do you want to start at the present and work your way backward?''

I hadn't considered that. He stood patiently waiting for my answer. ''What do you think?'' I asked anxiously.

''At the beginning, I think,'' he said promptly. ''Other considerations aside, it seems to me that starting with the present would be like reading a book from back to front. Intriguing, but not apt to make much sense.''

Our laughter mingled as he took me behind the counter and seated me at an ancient library table that stood against the back wall. After taking a number of what looked to be oversized scrapbooks from a shelf, he selected one and laid it before me. ''The *Bulletin* was founded in 1851, two years after the first gold was discovered here. They were a pretty wild bunch in those days.'' He opened the book for me.

''Are you sure I won't be a bother?'' I asked. I didn't know what I would have done had he replied that I would be, but such were the demands of polite society.

''Of course not. I have some writing to do, but my powers of concentration are enormous.'' With that he returned to the rolltop desk, and I began to search the first pages of the newspapers.

Though 1851 seemed a good place to start, since it was most probably the year of my birth, I had no idea of what I was looking for. I had no name, no incident, no familial belongings except for the emerald ring, on which to base my search, and I soon found that I was at least going to have to scan each story to see whether it could possibly connect to me. This was not as time-consuming as it would appear, since the early papers were no more than a single sheet folded in the middle and printed on all four sections, and a good deal of that space was taken up by advertisements. Besides, it was fascinating. There were tales of fabulous nuggets being found, of rich strikes in the area, of knife fights and lynchings, of businesses opening and expanding with incredible rapidity. The bald, factual accounts of even the most grisly stories added to their shocking impact. One account, that of a Chinaman who drowned himself in the creek because some drunken rowdies had cut off his pigtail, particularly touched me; another, of a miner found dead in a mining shack, intrigued me chiefly because it raised more questions than it answered. The long-ago scribe hinted darkly that the man had been brought there and deliberately left to die, and stridenly decried the lack of law and order in the burgeoning town. He did not, however, offer any solution to the murder or the lawlessness.

I read on, only vaguely aware that at his desk Mr. Newcomb was scribbling furiously. The murder victim, if indeed that is what he was, immediatley dropped from the *Bulletin*'s pages to make way for news of a particularly rich strike by a partnership of four men, one of whom was named Soames. I thought of the banker as he had sat behind his desk, the heavy jowls blurring the short jawline, the pudgy fingers clasping and unclasping the pen with which he had registered my account. It was difficult to imagine those same hands toughened and calloused from wielding a shovel, that now-corpulent body lean and hard from the arduous labor that must have accompanied the search for gold.

It was in the same edition that one article caused me to gasp with surprise. Mr. Newcomb looked up from his work.

"Are some of the town skeletons rattling in their closets?"

"It's an article about Miss Winfield. It mentions that she temporarily closed her saloon, the Red Garter."

"You find that surprising?" The intense eyes were regarding me with some puzzlement.

"Oh, not that she closed it. It's just that—it is hard to picture the owner of that fabulous mansion as the proprietor of a drinking and gambling establishment."

"And the secret backer of several respectable businesses."

"Then was she a—a—" I searched about for a genteel expression.

"A woman of ill repute? Not that I have heard. She was simply a beautiful lady with an astonishing business acumen."

"I see." I turned back to the article in the paper. This time her partner's name caught my attention. "And this Mr. Hannaford. Could he be related to a Marcus Hannaford?"

Jared smiled. "Ah, you have met Marcus, have you? Jake was his father. He died sometime before I came to Bittercreek. By then Miss Winfield had long since sold out to him and built the house on the rise."

"She must have been a good businesswoman. I wouldn't have expected a saloonkeeper to retire in such grandeur."

The look he cast me had a twinkle in it. "Neither did anyone else. Furthermore, she retained a number of friendships with important people in the town, at least of the male gender. The ladies seemed reluctant to clutch her to their bosoms and did so only under a good deal of duress, I suspect."

"You speak in the past tense. I know she no longer lives in the mansion, but has she died?"

"About five months ago. Except for the servants, the house has stood empty ever since."

I stared at the newspaper article again, but I wasn't seeing it. I was remembering the terror that had engulfed me as I had stood in the darkness before the mansion last night.

"How did she die?" I was almost reluctant to ask it.

"No one really knows, unless it is the servants and Doc Gentry. It was totally unexpected. The death certificate said heart failure, but we all die of that, don't we? In the long run?"

CHAPTER THREE

THOUGH HE SPOKE LIGHTLY, something in the editor's words sent a chill over me. I closed the scrapbook. So many of its stories dealt with death and violence. I felt a sudden deep distaste and didn't want to go on reading.

Jared, too, set aside his work.

"I generally close the office between twelve and one," he said, "but you're welcome to stay on if you like."

I glanced in surprise at the large wall clock. The hands indeed stood at twelve. Hastily, I rose. "No, thank you. I've had quite enough history for the moment. Though I would like to come back, if I may."

He escorted me to the door. "I'll look forward to it."

I went out, and he gave me another smile and wave through the clear glass pane of the office window.

As I returned the short distance to the hotel, I noticed that several passersby cast me glances of suspicion and annoyance. I held my head high and marched along with an air of studied indifference, but I knew my cheeks were bright with color. Why had I not ventured to ask Jared Newcomb the reason for the townspeople's strange attitude? As newspaper editor, he would be the one most likely to understand the inner workings of this insulated little town.

I entered the hotel lobby with a vast sense of relief and started directly upstairs. The newspaper scrapbooks had been dusty; my hands felt gritty, and I suspected that I had a smudge or two of dirt across my cheek. But as I reached the steps, I noticed that a man at the desk with Mr. Harper was covertly watching me. It was Mr. Soames. Thinking that he had brought my bankbook, I changed direction and started toward him. He seemed suddenly flustered, and with a quick word to the elderly hotel owner, slipped through the doors to the dining room.

I stopped at the desk. "Wasn't that Mr. Soames?" I asked. I was puzzled by the banker's behavior. It had seemed as though he had deliberately avoided me.

"What if 'twas?" Mr. Harper returned sharply.

"I left something in the bank. I thought he might have returned it." My voice held a dignified reprimand, and perhaps not unconsciously I brought my ring hand to rest on the edge of the counter. The gesture wasn't wasted. Mr. Harper's eyes dropped to the emerald and stayed there for a long moment.

"Well, he didn't." He spoke in the same truculent tone, but it was as though his attention had been diverted. He brought his gaze back to mine with an effort. "Just wanted a word with me, was all."

I was sure that their conversation had had to do with me, and I went to look in at the open doors to the dining room. Mr. Soames was not to be seen, but the street door was just closing gently. Feeling uneasy and somewhat upset, I strode past the hotel owner, who was still watching me, and went to my room.

I had meant only to tidy myself a bit, but once upstairs, I decided to change into something cooler, a gown of thin white lawn sprinkled with small green sprigs. I had been right about the smudges on my face, I saw as I peered in the mirror, and before dressing, I took off the emerald ring and bathed thoroughly. The china pitcher had been refilled, and I noticed belatedly that the bed had been freshly made. Whatever Mr. Harper's animosities toward me, they apparently didn't influence his sense of duty toward a paying guest.

I had just finished redressing my hair in a softer style and tying it with a green satin ribbon to match the one at my waist when there came a gentle rap at the door. I paused, one hand arrested in the act of smoothing a last curl. Who could it be? That quiet knock had not been made by the hand of Mr. Harper. Jared, perhaps? Or possibly Ellie, from the dining room, though I supposed she would be busy right now.

The knock came again, and I tucked the strand of hair into place and went with some reluctance to the door. I opened it cautiously, then swung it wide with a rush of relief.

Marcus was standing there, smiling. One well-manicured hand held my bankbook.

If he was surprised by the warmth of my greeting, he gave no indication of it. And I, having been momentarily overwhelmed by the sight of a friendly face, could find no graceful way to return to my former aloofness. "Oh," I exclaimed quickly to cover my confusion, "you have brought my bankbook. How nice of you, and how stupid of me to have left it!"

"It was a pleasure, and a perfect excuse for me to meet you again." His eyes were frankly admiring, and I thought he took particular note of the fact that the width of the ribbon across my waist was no more than the span of his hands. I waited until his eyes met mine again.

"I would invite you in," I said, "but I'm afraid it would hardly be considered proper."

"I have a better idea. May I take you to lunch? I surely deserve some recompense for returning your property to its rightful owner."

Though his tone held just the right mixture of warmth and gentlemanly cajolery, I was about to refuse when I remembered the coupling of Miss Winfield's name with that of his father. This man, I realized suddenly, must have been raised in Bittercreek and apparently still returned frequently. Perhaps he could help me find a link to my past. He might even, I thought with a sudden clutch of the heart, have known my real parents. No matter how dangerously handsome he was, I decided that I must risk it.

"I would like that," I said. "Just let me get my pocketbook."

DURING A LUNCHEON of cold roast chicken accompanied by tall, cool glasses of lemonade, I found the opportunity to ask Marcus about the strange behavior of the town's inhabitants.

"I have been puzzling about that," he said, "ever since Harper tried to refuse you the room. And I found the answer right under my nose. It's the will. Raven Winfield's will."

I stared at him. "But what on earth would that have to do with me? I never even knew her."

"Nothing, most likely. But the will states that her house and all her possessions, except for certain stipulated bequests, go to the town. Unless an heir—a direct descendant—appears before the designated six months have elapsed. That time is almost up."

A tiny chill went over me. "And you are saying that I—that they think that I—"

"Might be that heir, come to claim your inheritance." He smiled, and his hazel eyes lit up in a way that melted my bones. "But don't feel that you have been singled out. I'm sure that any stranger under forty would have been dealt the same treatment. For the next few weeks the climate of Bittercreek will hardly be receptive to unknown visitors."

Marcus went on with his chicken, but I couldn't swallow another bite. My first reaction was relief that I had confided in no one my reason for being there, for I realized immediately that it was possible—just barely possible—that I did indeed bear a relationship to Miss Winfield. After all, someone had chosen just this time to hint at my past connections to the town.

"You're not eating," Marcus said with sudden concern. "Don't you find the chicken to your liking?"

"Oh! Oh, yes, it's delicious. It's just that... Well, I think your story is fascinating. You say it must be a direct descendant who inherits. Did Miss Winfield have many children?"

"One daughter—an only child. The story is a sad one. Rose, the daughter, left very suddenly in 1851 for San Francisco, purportedly to visit friends. She was never heard from again."

Once more I felt that little touch of chill. "How awful! Surely they tried to find her!"

"For years, I think. Rose was just seventeen, and her mother could never accept the fact that she had probably met some misfortune and would not be coming back. She is even provided for in the will."

I visualized Raven Winfield living all alone in that huge house, wandering restlessly from room to room, waiting, forever waiting, for the beloved daughter who would never come. A vast, all-pervading sadness washed over me, and I felt the sting of tears. Marcus reached across the table and covered my cold hand with his.

"Don't look like that," he said. "It was a happy delusion. In every other way Miss Winfield was the sharpest lady I have ever known. If she chose to think that Rose would return one day, where was the harm? It kept her satisfied until the end."

My thoughts had returned to my own possible part in this. "If Rose disappeared twenty years ago, she would now be thirty-seven, wouldn't she?" I felt relief, yet disappointment at the thought. "Then why on earth would people be suspicious of me?"

His smile turned a little quizzical. "Are you sure you can't figure out the answer to that?"

And, of course, I could. If she hadn't died immediately, Rose might have had a child, and anyone my
age or younger could be that child. To hide my agitation, I picked up my glass of lemonade and noticed
that my hand was trembling.

"Are you sure you're all right?" Marcus asked with
concern. "You look a little pale."

I *felt* a little pale. It was farfetched to think that I,
a nameless waif brought up under the onus of charity, could be heiress to that fabulous mansion and the
appreciable wealth that no doubt accompanied it. Yet
I realized that given the year of my rescue from the fire
and the fact that it took place in San Francisco, it was
within the realm of possibility. And while my foster
father had told me many times that he had made in-
numerable fruitless inquires about my family and my
past, I wondered, not for the first time, how my benefactor had known where to find me after all those
years. Must I assume that my foster father, the one
loving, caring person in my life, had been lying to me?

I tried to dismiss the possibility from my mind.

"May we go outside?" I asked Marcus tremu-
lously. I was having difficulty breathing. "I feel in
need of some air."

"Of course." He rose hastily. "Are you sure you
wouldn't like to return to your room?"

"No, please. I think perhaps it is the heat that is
affecting me. The weather is much cooler in San
Francisco."

Perhaps it really was the heat, for the atmosphere of
the dining room was close and still. But I thought it
more likely that it was the sudden weight of suspicion

that was troubling me. Once outside, I leaned against the porch railing and fought to regain my breath.

"Better?" Marcus asked sympathetically. "Though it is no wonder you have difficulty when you lace yourself so tightly."

It was hardly a gentlemanly thing to say, and as a lady, I shouldn't have deigned to answer. But his words touched my small vanity. I retorted indignantly, "I do not wear corsets! My waist is naturally small!" and then blushed to see the teasing smile touch his eyes. It served to distract me from my thoughts, and I found that I could breathe quite normally again. "I'm sorry," I said then. "I didn't mean to spoil your lunch."

He shrugged and dismissed it. "Perhaps I should apologize. All my talk of deaths and wills may have upset you."

"Oh, no!" I protested hastily. "Raven's Rise has intrigued me ever since I arrived in Bittercreek. I hope you will tell me more of its history."

"I'll do better than that. Would you like a guided tour? I had planned to go over there this afternoon, anyway. That is," he amended in some alarm, "if you think you are up to it."

I knew that I had gone pale again. "Oh, please," I said. "It is just excitement. I never dreamed that I would actually get to go inside."

AS WE WALKED the short distance to Raven's Rise, Marcus told me how he happened to have a key to the mansion. "My father and Miss Winfield were long-time friends," he said, "and she had made him one of the executors of her estate. When he died, she replaced his name with mine. Since the six months the will stipulated are almost up, I decided it was time I came back and began settling her affairs."

"I see. Then if someone were to claim to be the missing heir, he or she would have to bring proof to you."

"Or to Doc Gentry. He is the other executor."

I digested this in silence. A gambler's son and a country doctor seemed strange choices for executors of an estate the size that Miss Winfield's must be. But perhaps I presumed there. Marcus had not specifically said that there was a great deal of money involved. Boldly, I asked him about it.

"She had made some sensible investments," he said somewhat guardedly, "and there is a tidy amount in the local bank. But it hardly seems enough to account for the avarice the people in this town are exhibiting, though certainly the house would make a handsome and imposing city hall."

We were approaching the gate in the iron fence. I said, "My first impression was of a queen looking reprovingly down upon her subjects from the royal throne."

"That has occurred to most of the citizens of Bittercreek," Marcus remarked with a trace of irony. "It did little to add to her popularity."

I felt my heart pound with both excitement and unease as we went up the steep, winding walk toward the house; its many small-paned windows seemed to be watching us with surprise and disapproval. The exterior of the mansion was a flat, lusterless gray; the various tortured trim boards were painted a darker, sterner color that made them appear to be eyebrows pulled down in a forbidding frown. Behind the shining panes of glass, spotless white lace curtains hung motionless. In one large bay a fern stood on a wicker stand, its foliage so perfect, that it seemed unreal. The porch and steps were free of even one errant leaf from the surrounding oaks, and the door brass was spotless and shining, yet it was as though the house had stood entirely empty for a long time. I felt a somber, silent waiting emanate from the place.

The ornate brass key that Marcus drew from his pocket turned easily in the lock. He pushed the door open, and we stepped into the wide entry hall.

The polished wood floor shone as though overlaid with water. Along one wall was a narrow table above which hung an ornate gilt mirror. A pair of painted china oil lamps, their clear glass chimneys free of the slightest speck of dust, were at each end of the table. Against an opposite wall a straight-backed settle stood with uncompromising sternness, and just beyond, a wide, steep stair led to the floor above.

"Does someone live here?" I whispered. I had been prepared for thick dust and draperies of cobwebs. Uneasily, I looked toward the open doorways on either side of the hall.

"There are two servants. A couple," Marcus answered in a normal tone. "When Miss Winfield was alive, they stayed in the house. Just now they are occupying a cottage at the rear of the property." He, too, glanced about, but without my air of guilt. "You go

ahead and look around. I'll just step out and tell them
that we're here.''

After he had gone, I stood quite still for a moment,
trying to get a sense of the house and perhaps of the
woman who had lived in it, but again there was only
an air of quiet waiting. Slowly, I moved to the nearest
doorway and looked in.

I felt a sudden shock. The square, high-ceilinged
room, evidently the parlor, was simply bursting with
"things." Each upholstered chair and the padded set-
tee were flanked by polished wooden tables whose tops
were cluttered with trinkets of all descriptions. China
figures, miniature portraits, wooden carvings, filigreed fans, glass darning eggs, gold-chased paper-
weights, lamps with elaborate silk shades and dangling
crystal beads or with china bowls so heavily hand
painted that the rose petals stood out as though real,
all vied for space on every available surface. A rosewood secretary, its leaded glass doors open, displayed
small fluted cups and matching teapot. Delicate porcelain figurines danced the minuet across the mahogany mantel above a marble fireplace front. In one
corner of the room, a tall vase held iridescent ostrich
plumes. And on every available wall space, hanging
from faded velvet ribbons attached to the picture rail
above, were photographs and paintings in elaborate
gilt frames.

In spite of the clutter, my eyes were almost immediately drawn to the painting above the mantel. It was
very large and the only object in this room that had
been allowed to stand apart. The empty space surrounding it brought it inevitably to my attention.

The portrait was of a woman and a child, the latter not more than ten or eleven. Both people were beautiful. The mother had fine patrician features, and the arms that embraced the child were slim and delicate. Her eyes, large and dark beneath black wings of shining hair, glowed with love and pride. The daughter's russet head nestled in the curve of her mother's slender neck, and one arm, still with the slight chubbiness of childhood, reached up to embrace her; but there was in the girl's expression an air of hauteur, or willful possessiveness, that somehow was disquieting.

I had an overpowering urge to examine the picture more closely. Moving with a trancelike languor, I went to stand directly beneath it. The painter had done his work well. I thought that I could almost pick up the satin ribbon that flowed from the child's hair, the delicate lace of the handkerchief held in the mother's slender fingers.

I stared and felt my breath catch in my throat. From one slim finger came the rich glow of emerald green. As the room seemed to sway around me, I brought my own hand up and saw that my ring was gone; dimly, I remembered removing it in my room at the hotel. I looked again at the painting. There was no mistaking it. The emerald in the portrait was the very one that I had been wearing only an hour or so ago.

The room grew hazy, and the strength seemed to drain from my knees. Then, from directly behind me, a voice said ominously, "Who are you? How dare you sneak in here and meddle about with Miss Raven's things?"

I swung around. Standing there was a tall, thin woman dressed all in black, from the turban that completely covered her hair to the sensible shoes whose polished tips protruded from beneath the voluminous folds of her heavy skirt. Yellow cat's eyes glared with rage above prominent cheekbones over which shiny brown hair was tightly stretched. As I stared, she took a step nearer.

"Well?" she demanded threateningly. "What d'you have to say for yourself?"

I tried to answer her, but I couldn't make my voice obey me. The room was still swaying, the haze increasing. I felt my legs weaken and buckle. The last things I remembered were the cat's eyes widening in surprise and her forward movement as the flowered carpet rose to meet me.

CHAPTER FOUR

LANGUIDLY, I OPENED MY EYES. I was lying on a sofa, and Marcus was bending over me, gently chafing my icy hands. Anxiety clouded his face, and as I struggled to sit up, he said quickly, "No, no, lie still. Dulcie has gone for a glass of water. You just rest for a few minutes."

I obeyed without a murmur. To tell the truth, I felt both strangely weak and mentally befuddled. I could not quite grasp what had happened or how I had come to be lying in a room I was sure I had never seen before.

Unlike the cluttered parlor, the room was serene and dignified. Comfortable upholstered furniture stood invitingly about, and shelves of leather-bound volumes lined the room. There were lamps with translucent shades placed close to the deep chairs flanking the fireplace; only a few tasteful pieces of porcelain and brass broke the open expanse of the polished tables.

I glanced at the large portrait over the mantel and could not look away.

Again, it was the woman with the patrician features and wings of shining hair, but this time she was alone. The dark and obscure background against which she stood and her black, lusterless gown served to emphasize the glow of face, slender neck and bare ivory shoulders. One delicate hand lay against the softly rounded breast. The other was almost hidden in the folds of the bell-like skirt, but on the tapered finger— I gave a sharp, involuntary intake of breath. In this portrait, as in the parlor, she was wearing the ornate emerald ring with the circlet of diamonds, which was even now lying on the washstand in my room at the hotel.

"What—!" Marcus exclaimed, and smothered a startled oath. "You've gone white as a ghost again! You can't be as strong as you look, Miss Ames. Unless..." His words trailed off, and he turned to look up at the picture over the mantel.

The servant woman chose that moment to return with a glass of water, thus earning my undying gratitude.

"I've sent Hiram to fetch Doc Gentry," she told Marcus. Then, to me, almost grudgingly she said, "It wasn't my intent to startle you like that. How was I to know you'd been invited by Mr. Hannaford?"

"It—it's quite all right," I managed. Marcus had helped me to a sitting position, and I sipped the water gratefully. "And I really don't need the doctor. It's just that—" I stopped, realizing that I could not give an adequate explanation without revealing my possession of the ring.

"I'll be the judge of that, young lady," Dr. Gentry said from the doorway. He came in and pulled a chair close to the sofa, then opened his black leather bag and hauled out a worn stethoscope. "There must be some explanation for your keeling over like that, though I'll admit Dulcie can sneak up on a person quiet as a cat." He put the stethoscope to his ears and placed the other end at the approximate area of my heart. "Hmm," he said after a long moment. "A little faster than should be, mebbe, but it's tripping along steady as a clock." He examined my eyes and the inside of my mouth, then leaned back and took the stethoscope from around his neck. "Sound as a dollar. But I'd suggest taking it easy for the rest of the afternoon."

"I'll see to that," Marcus said firmly. "I'll take her back to the hotel right away. We can explore the house another time."

I murmured something by way of apology and disappointment, but I was secretly relieved. The shock of seeing the emerald ring—my ring—on Raven Winfield's finger was still with me, and I wanted most desperately to be alone to think the matter through and consider all of its ramifications. Besides, I had discovered that fainting, no matter the reason, does leave one feeling rather weak and fragile, and it was not unpleasant to have Marcus and the others hover around me, pressing me with concerned attention. In fact, I enjoyed it all immensely. In my foster mother's house I had been, as she had termed it, quite 'rudely' healthy and had not required her gentle ministrations, in part, I suspect, because I had known they wouldn't be forthcoming. So I made the most of the moment and during our journey relied on the strength of Marcus's arm rather more than I actually needed to.

He insisted on escorting me to the very door of my room.

"You will rest?" he asked.

I felt a warm pleasure mixed with guilt at the concern in his voice. "Of course," I said, "but I really am all right now. It is very unlike me to be beset by feminine vapors."

"I would have assumed so from the tenor of our first meeting." Marcus's eyes held their usual mild amusement and something more. "The other Selina was staunchly independent; this one seems rather more soft and yielding." He ran an index finger down the curve of my jaw, allowing it to rest just beneath the point of my slightly cleft chin. "It doesn't disturb me to see that there are two of you. I find you both delightful."

The delicious warmth that had stirred in me grew and spread throughout my body, and I knew that it must reflect in my face, but Marcus didn't take advantage of it. As I watched him go toward the stairs with his long, graceful stride, I could still feel his gentle touch along my cheek.

Once in my room, I went immediatley to the washstand. While I knew beyond a doubt that my emerald and that in the portrait were one and the same, I wanted to hold it in my hand, to confirm this irrefutable link between the waif Selina and that regal and lovely mistress of Raven's Rise.

But the ring was not there. The washstand stood barren; empty.

At first I could not take it in. Then, with a cry of anguished disbelief, I surged forward, unwilling to believe the evidence of my eyes. Frantically, I moved pitcher and washbasin, emptied the pitcher's contents into the bowl and dropped to my knees to search the flowered carpet surrounding the washstand. My straining eyes and groping fingers encountered nothing.

Hysteria rose in me, and I sat back on my heels and closed my eyes in an effort to fight it. "Be calm," I told myself sternly. "It must be here. You probably picked it up yourself and put it down again when Marcus came." But though I forced myself to search thoroughly and systematically in every corner and crevice of the room, I knew that I wouldn't find it. Someone had slipped into this room and stolen it while I had been out with Marcus.

A wave of giddiness passed over me, and I dropped into the wooden rocker. Who could have done such a thing? Nothing else had been touched; I had noted that during my search. Nor had the door been tampered with. The intruder had to have been someone with easy access to this room.

Ellie? I could not believe that it was she. Something in her straightforward glance denied the possibility of such underhandedness; besides, she would neither dare to wear the ring nor be able to dispose of it easily, and she would be the first one suspected. If there were other hirelings, I had not seen evidence of them and assumed that Mr. Harper did much of the work himself.

Harper. What had he and Soames been discussing in the lobby this noon? I remembered that they both had clearly noted the ring, though the banker's interest had been the sharper. In fact, his expression upon seeing it had almost been—I searched for the elusive word—recognition.

I felt a sudden burst of comprehension. Of course. He had known Raven from the beginning. He had to have seen her wear the emerald or, barring that, seen it in her portrait. He must have suspected that I was her heir. Had he inveigled Mr. Harper into spiriting away what was possibly my only evidence to it?

I had no way of proving my suspicions, but I knew with a sudden, furious certainty that they were founded on fact. I leaped from the rocker and paced the room, trying to control the rage and disappointment that threatened to engulf me. For without the ring no one would be willing to believe that I was indeed Raven Winfield's granddaughter and heir to her considerable fortune.

I stopped my frantic pacing and stared blindly out the single window. A blur of tears filmed my eyes, and angrily I dashed them away. Did those men really know what they had done to me? My financial problems would have been over—not a small thing to a young woman cast, as I had been, into the world to make her own way. Society was not kind to a female in that position; men considered her ripe for exploitation, and women feared her influence over their husbands.

I knew it was useless to confront the two men with my suspicions, so I must find some other way to convince Marcus Hannaford and the doctor that I was indeed Raven Winfield's granddaughter. Marcus, I thought, would be predisposed to believe me, but Dr. Gentry and the townspeople would doubtless require a good deal of convincing. Unless I could present some evidence, some fact, that would corroborate my story, their animosity could well turn to dangerous resentment.

The only way I could think to search for this information was by continuing to look through the past editions of the *Bittercreek Bulletin*.

I glanced quickly at the clock. If I hurried, I might reach its office in time to spend an hour or so among the scrapbooks. But as I started for the door, another wave of dizziness passed over me. I clutched the bedpost, then eased myself down upon the quilted coverlet. Perhaps the doctor had been right in his prescription; I decided that a few moment's rest would not delay my search unduly.

WHEN I AWOKE, the room had grown dim, and there was a soft rapping at the door. I sat up and slid to the edge of the bed, then stood gingerly. The weakness seemed to have passed. Hearing a second knock, I went to answer it.

Ellie Henderson stood in the hall. She held a tray set with covered dishes.

"I hope I didn't wake you," she said, "but Mr. Hannaford told me that if you hadn't come to dinner by seven, I was to bring something up. He explained that you were feeling a mite under the weather."

"How thoughtful of him!" I was warmed once again by this evidence of his consideration. "Please. Bring it in, will you?" I lit the lamp as she entered and placed the footed tray on a nearby table.

"Would you have me set it out here, or do you want to get into bed and eat it?" she inquired.

"Oh, please, set it out." The concern in her expression deepened my conviction that she had had nothing to do with the disappearance of my ring. "You will have me convinced I'm an invalid if this keeps up. I just had a bit of a fright this afternoon, that's all."

"It isn't any wonder, in that spooky old house." Ellie shuddered convincingly. "You couldn't get me to go in there for anything."

"Why?" I took my seat in the straight chair she had drawn to the table. "Is it supposed to be haunted?" I was deeply interested in hearing her answer, but Ellie, I saw, thought I was making fun of her.

"You may laugh if you like, but there have been peculiar goings-on in that place. Lights fluttering here and there in the dead of night and creaks and moans from where no one ought to be. There's many a strong man in this town that wouldn't go near the Rise after dark for a twenty-dollar gold piece."

I was struck by the reproach in her tone and hastened to reassure her. "I wasn't laughing at you, Ellie. I was just curious, that's all. Has anyone asked the servants about the lights?"

"That Dulcie and Hiram don't mingle with the townfolk. The way they march around with their noses in the air, you'd think they owned the mansion instead of Miss Winfield. But I did hear that they told Mayor Ogilvey they didn't know any more about it than anyone else. And Hiram let it be known he stands watch with a shotgun many a night."

I shivered a little. I hadn't yet seen Hiram, but something in Ellie's tone indicated that he alone should have discouraged any intruder.

After promising to come back for the tray and dishes, Ellie stood hesitantly at my door. "I don't mean to bother you," she began, "but are you still wanting ma's spare room? She said she'd be proud to have you."

I had forgotten all about it. "Oh, Ellie, I'm sorry!" I exclaimed. "This ridiculous fainting spell has thrown it right out of my mind." I thought rapidly. Until I knew how my claim was going to be received, it would hardly be fair to embroil the Hendersons in it. "I think I'd better wait for a while. I may not be staying in town as long as I had thought." Her face fell, and I added hastily, "Though I would like very much to meet your mother. Might I call on her tomorrow afternoon?"

She brightened. "She'd like that. I think it was the chance of a good gossip she was looking forward to more than anything."

I smiled and said, "I'd like that, too." After Ellie had gone, I reflected that her mother might, indeed, be a mine of information. If I knew the right questions to ask.

IT WAS ALL that I could do to wait until nine the next morning before appearing at the newspaper office. As before, Jared Newcomb was working at his desk. Upon my arrival, he rose quickly and greeted me with his unrestrained enthusiasm.

"Miss Ames! I hadn't dared hope for a return visit from you so soon. Have you come to take another look at the town's tempestuous history?"

"While I am here, perhaps." I had thought of a plausible excuse for this present visit while walking from the hotel. "Actually, I came to amend the address of my subscription. I plan to stay on at the hotel a while longer."

His heavy eyebrows rose. "You didn't find the Henderson place to your liking?"

"Oh, it isn't that! It's just that I may be leaving town soon, after all."

"I see." He drew a blank pad to him and made a notation. "I'm sorry to hear that. I had hoped to interview you for the newspaper. It isn't often that we have such a charming young lady visit us." He smiled coaxingly. "Would you be willing to tell me something about yourself and the purpose of your stay in Bittercreek? I might still make this week's edition."

"Oh, no!" I heard the alarm in my voice and tried to temper it. "Please. It would be of no interest to anyone, and I would find it uncomfortable to have such attention drawn to me." He looked so disappointed that I added impulsively, "Truly, I don't have a noteworthy past. But if anything of consequence develops concerning me, I promise you will be the first to know."

The intense blue eyes probed mine; then his lips curled in an odd little smile. "I'll have to be satisfied with that, I suppose. And the word of a lady is as good as gold." With that he lifted the gate and ushered me back to the library table. I was relieved to see that he was not going to pursue the matter further.

Jared again brought out the 1851 set of back issues. I leafed through them until I found where I had left off at the account of the murdered miner. I turned to the next edition. After reading a few words of the lead story, I felt the hair on my nape begin to stir. For in it Raven Winfield, whom I now thought of as my grandmother, accused Soames and his partners of murdering that same miner, stealing his strike, which they named the Four Horsemen Mine, and claiming it for their own!

Fascinated, I read on. The miner, Will Prentiss, had been a close friend of Raven's (the article implied rather more than that), and she swore that he had told her of the strike shortly before he was killed. He had been on his way to register his claim, she declared, when he had been waylaid and left to die in that deserted cabin. She demanded that the four men be arrested and brought to justice.

Soames and his partners protested vehemently, according to the account, but the circumstances *had* been odd. Until a few days before his death, Will Prentiss had been a member of the partnership and had vowed, with the others, that any gold found was to be shared equally among the five. But there had been a bitter quarrel, and Will had left the group and struck out on his own. A few days later, he had been found dead. Not long after that, Soames and his friends had announced the discovery of the richest strike in Bittercreek history. It had seemed suspicious, but it was simply Raven's word against the partners', and there the matter had stalemated.

I quickly scanned the following editions. The murder had again made headlines. Raven now declared that she had uncovered a witness and demanded an inquiry. When it was held, however, she had been unable to produce the promised witness, and the charges had been dropped.

I felt a vast disappointment. Though the affair could have had nothing to do with me, it did involve my grandmother, and I had been eager to learn the truth of it. Now, it seemed, I never would. But as I dispiritedly scanned the remaining articles, one small item near the back caught my attention and sent the murder completely from my mind. It reported that the town assayer, one Henry Ames, with his wife and family, had mysteriously departed from Bittercreek in the dead of night, leaving no indication of their destination.

I sat still as a stone, but my blood was racing. My eyes were riveted to that name. Henry Ames. A vision of him rose in my mind: kind, smiling, the only member of my foster family who truly accepted me. He had spent as much time as he could with me without incurring the wrath of his wife, but in all those years he had never mentioned that he had once lived in Bittercreek.

Quietly, I closed the book.

"You are through already?" Jared remarked. I had forgotten his existence.

"For today." I tried to smile, but my face felt frozen. "Thank you."

"Anytime," he said. I saw that he was looking at me strangely. "Would you like me to escort you back to the hotel?"

"No," I replied. "I'm quite all right." I rose carefully and left the office.

I have no memory of my return to the hotel. I must have walked through the lobby, up the stairs. I must have fumbled in my pocketbook for my key, opened my door and gone in. I must have shut it carefully behind me. And I must have sunk into the comfort of the rocking chair, for I found myself, a long time later, swaying gently in its rigid embrace. My whole being was concentrated on that one piece of knowledge that had leaped at me from the pages of the *Bulletin*.

In 1851, Henry Ames had lived in Bittercreek. He had known my grandmother, had known Rose, had no doubt known Dr. Gentry and even the boy Marcus Hannaford. He had surfaced in San Francisco in time to save a baby, daughter of Rose, from death in an apartment-house fire and had taken her into his home despite his wife's protests.

At last I understood why my foster mother hated me. Henry Ames was my natural father.

CHAPTER FIVE

ONCE I HAD PUZZLED IT OUT, I knew without question that it was true, just as I had, upon seeing the emerald ring, known absolutely that I was indeed Rose's daughter.

I also realized that I did not have a good opinion of my mother, who had apparently pursued a married man to San Francisco without caring a whit that in doing so she had broken Raven's heart. That haughty, superior air of the child in the portrait had evidently carried over into young adulthood. I felt that by her willfulness she had not only hurt her mother but had deprived me of the warm and loving relationships for which I had so longed. She had probably, I thought with passionate anger, even stolen Raven's emerald ring.

But what of Henry Ames? Painful as it was to me to criticize the only person I had ever loved, honesty forced me to admit that he had hardly played a heroic part in all of it. He, a respectable married man, had obviously had dalliance with a girl of seventeen and gotten her pregnant. Why else had he fled under cover of night? And he had continued to see her in San Francisco, for it was entirely too providential that he had been passing by at the time of the apartment-house fire.

It puzzled me, though, that after Rose's death he had not brought me back to my grandmother. Surely that would have been the kindest and most sensible thing. It would have assuaged Raven's grief while giving me a loving home and spared both him the necessity of foisting me off on his resentful wife and me the shame of being reared as a charity child.

At last the tears, dammed from early childhood, began slipping down my cheeks. Whether they were caused by the relief of knowing at last my true origins or because I mourned the happiness I had been cheated of, I didn't know.

"Oh, father," I wept aloud at last, "couldn't you have done the honorable thing and acknowledged me? At least then I would have known that the name I bore was truly mine!"

FINALLY, drained though I was by emotion, a sense of peace stole over me. I knew my identity. I was Selina Ames, daughter of Rose, daughter of Henry. And, I thought with determination, granddaughter of Raven Winfield.

A sudden energy flowed through me. I arose and began repairing my disheveled and tear-stained appearance. As I did so, my mind was working rapidly. If Raven had appointed Marcus and Dr. Gentry as executors, they must have known her well. Surely they would recognize the validity of my claim. They might even have facts unknown to me that would corroborate my story. I had no idea where either of them might be found this time of day, but surely someone downstairs would be able to tell me. Someone, I amended, besides Mr. Harper. I felt a choking anger at the mere thought of speaking to him.

But when I reached the lobby, I had cause to change my mind. It was something in the way he watched me covertly as I descended the last few steps, then turned hastily to fumble among the objects on the back counter as though unaware of my approach. I felt the color rise in my cheeks, my breath come quickly. With stiffened spine and what I hoped was regal dignity, I went directly to the desk.

"Mr. Harper," I commanded when he didn't turn to face me. "I would like to speak with you. I wish to register a complaint."

He turned reluctantly. It seemed to me that his manner was the embodiment of guilt. His eyes didn't quite meet mine.

"If the room ain't to your likin', you can move on," he said with an attempt at his usual belligerence.

"You have a thief in your hotel, Mr. Harper." I deliberately made my voice clear and carrying and had the satisfaction of seeing heads turn. "I am missing a valuable ring. I would appreciate your directing me to the police station so that I may report it."

"Now hold on." Mr. Harper looked alarmed. "How do you know it's been stole? Mebbe you just mislaid it, or mebbe you lost it someplace besides my hotel. Anyhow, the sheriff's out of town. Won't be back until tomorrow."

"I see. In that case, the thief has until then to return my property. He would be most wise if he were to take advantage of it.'' Pretending to be serenely oblivious to his sputterings, I sailed out the door and onto the porch of the hotel.

As I had spoken to Mr. Harper, I had been vaguely aware of someone watching me from the door of the dining room. I realized now that it had been Ellie, for she hurried from the dining room's outer door to intercept me. Her eyes were bright with unshed tears.

"Oh, Miss Ames, I do hope you don't think it was me that did it! If Mr. Harper suspects it for a minute, I'll lose my job—and I don't know what ma and I will do if that happens!"

She was obviously frightened, and I felt immediate remorse. I put my arm around her and drew her away from the entrance to the hotel. "Oh, Ellie, of course I don't suspect you." I lowered my voice. "As a matter of fact, I think I know who did it, and I'm quite sure Mr. Harper has a good idea of it, too."

Ellie breathed a quick, sharp sigh of relief. "Thank the Lord! Will you tell my mother so when you go to see her today? Mayor Ogilvey's wife was in the lobby, and it'll be all over town in an hour."

Again I had forgotten Mrs. Henderson and my promise visit. I hesitated, but seeing Ellie's anxious face, I decided that my confrontation with Marcus and Dr. Gentry would have to wait.

"I'll go right now, Ellie," I said, "if you think that will be convenient for your mother. Which is your house?"

She pointed out a neat white cottage near Raven's Rise, then hurried back inside. I crossed the street and started toward it, conscious as always of the mansion's brooding presence.

Mrs. Henderson was an ample, friendly sort of person and was obviously pleased that I had chosen to visit her. She first ushered me into the parlor, but when she discovered that I had not yet had lunch, insisted that I follow her into the kitchen for a sandwich and a cup of tea. "I do think," she said after getting me settled at the large oilcloth-covered table, "that the best visits are in the kitchen, anyhow. Seems as a body can lean on their elbows and get right down to things."

Suddenly I was glad for my sake as well as Ellie's that I had postponed my meeting with Marcus and Dr. Gentry. If Ellie's mother knew as much about the town as I suspected she did, I might have more facts with which to convince them of the validity of my claim to Raven's Rise. But I was at a loss as to how I might bring the subject up.

Mrs. Henderson solved that problem for me. After I had eaten, she said, "Ellie tells me you mightn't be staying in Bittercreek, after all. I wouldn't wonder. There's not much to offer a body. It beats me what keeps folks staying here. More tea?"

"Yes, please. I would think it might be a pleasant place to live."

She sighed. "A person would think so. But there's a kind of bad feeling in this town. And if you ask me, it's got something to do with that big old house up there." She nodded in the direction of Raven's Rise.

"Did you know Miss Winfield?" I ventured. "Or have you only moved here recently?"

"Gracious, no. I've been here since '55. Ellie's pa got himself killed right off in a mine accident, so I opened a boardinghouse. Kept it until the gold ran out." She leaned forward. "Miss Winfield loaned me the money and told me not to tell anyone. But every cent was paid back, and she's dead, so I guess it doesn't matter now."

"She sounds like a kind person." It was almost a protest, for I had been stung by her connecting Raven's Rise with a bad feeling in the town.

"Well, she was and she wasn't. Word gets around, and I know I'm not the only one she helped out. But anything Raven Winfield wanted to have happen in this town happened. And if she didn't want it to happen, such as another saloon or some business or other she didn't approve of, it didn't happen." Her round, uncomplicated face held a puzzled expression. "I never could figure it out. Seems like the important people in this town just broke their necks to please her, which is odd, her being a former saloonkeeper and all."

"Important people?"

She nodded. "Senator Bentley, Mayor Ogilvey—people like that."

I remembered Marcus's pointing out that a state senator still lived in Bittercreek. "I'm surprised the senator hasn't moved to Sacramento," I remarked.

"That's what I said. Why do any of 'em stay here? Especially when they're rich as Crocus, or whatever that fellow's name was." She passed me a plate of molasses cookies. "All three of them took a bundle out of the Horsemen before it petered out."

"All three of them? Senator Bentley and Mayor Ogilvey were part owners of the Four Horsemen Mine?"

She stirred her tea. "Along with Banker Soames."

"And the other partner?"

"Weren't any other as far as I know."

"But—the mine's name—"

"Oh, you mean the *Four* Horsemen." She thought about it. "Seems to me there was another one. I remember something about him drinking himself to death. But that was before Jim and I moved here."

All this was interesting, considering my grandmother's accusations of the three men, but I was learning nothing that would further my cause. I decided to take a chance.

"My foster father, Henry Ames, used to live in Bittercreek. Have you heard of him?"

"No, can't say as I have. What kind of work did he do?"

"He was an assayer when he lived here. I'm...not quite sure just what that is."

She laughed. "Times change, don't they? Twenty years ago an assayer was one of the most important men in this town. He was the fellow who looked at your ore and told you whether your claim was worth anything or not."

"And...Rose?" I asked tentatively. "Do you... happen to know anything about her?"

Mrs. Henderson's glance was suddenly keen. "Just what everybody else knows. She ran away to get out from under her mother's thumb and was never heard from again. Why? What should I know about her?"

Ellie's mother might be a simple woman, but she wasn't stupid. The bright blue eyes had narrowed a little, and I knew I would get no further information from her. Unless—

"Mrs. Henderson," I said with as much appeal as I could summon, "can you keep a secret?"

Her eyes did not light with the voraciousness of the inveterate talebearer. "Look, Miss Ames," she said flatly, "I enjoy a good gossip as well as the next one. But I stay away from the harmful kind, I don't pass on lies if I know it, and I never tell anything somebody tells me in confidence. Whether you believe that is up to you."

Somehow I did believe it. Besides, I had to explain about Ellie and the theft of my emerald ring.

"You see," I began, and though I tried my best to control it, my voice trembled, "I think I may be Raven Winfield's granddaughter."

Her eyes widened. "My land! No wonder you're asking questions. What makes you think so, anyhow?"

My explanation didn't take long, even including the part about the missing ring. "So you see," I concluded, "I have very little evidence to offer the executors, which is what those two men who stole my ring are counting on."

Mrs. Henderson seemed ready to believe my story, but she questioned me as to why I thought Soames had put Harper up to taking the ring. "Oh, it's easy to see why Harper would do what Soames wanted, seeing as the bank holds the mortgage on his hotel, but why would Mr. Soames care who ends up with Raven's

Rise? And it wouldn't do his bank any good to have him accused of a thing like that. As to the other, I wish I could help, but I never heard a thing about Rose and this Henry Ames."

I don't know what I had hoped for, but I felt forlorn as I took my leave. Most of the townspeople would not be as charitable as Ellie's mother, and for all I knew, when word of my claim got around, I might be ordered out of town on the next stage. Nevertheless, I decided to confront Marcus and Dr. Gentry with what evidence I had.

On my way back to the hotel, I passed a group of young boys playing marbles in the dusty street. One of them, a thin, wiry youngster, glanced up at me with a pleasant expression. On a sudden impulse I hailed him. He jumped up and came to me immediately.

"Do you know where Dr. Gentry's office is?" I asked.

"Sure. It's in his house. That peaky-roofed one, down there." He pointed past the hotel to the end of the street opposite Raven's Rise.

"I'd like you to take a message to him. Tell him that Selina Ames asks that he and Mr. Hannaford call on her at the hotel as soon as is convenient for them. Can you remember that?" As I spoke, I was reaching into my pocketbook for a coin. His eyes glowed at the sight of the nickel I offered him.

"Sure! Gee, thanks!" He took it and sped off down the street without a word to his fellow players.

Mr. Harper wasn't in the hotel lobby, and I crossed it without incident and went upstairs. My pulse quickened a little as I entered my room, but the washstand stood empty as before. My disappointment was followed immediately by self-disgust. Why had I supposed that my feeble attempt at coercion would bring results? The two men could simply deny any knowledge of the ring, and my accusations would go unheeded.

Fighting the bitterness that again threatened to overwhelm me, I tidied up both the room and my own appearance. Then, not knowing how much idle time stretched before me, I began a slow pace back and forth across the room.

I had taken no more than a few turns, however, when there came a decisive knock on the door. I flew to open it. Dr. Gentry was there, bag in hand. Behind him, looking serious and concerned, was Marcus Hannaford.

I stood silent a moment, aware of the strange fluttering at the base of my throat that had begun at the sight of Marcus. Then I said, "Please, gentlemen, won't you come in?"

Dr. Gentry put his bag on the table and turned a critical eye on me. "Feeling a bit peaked again, are you? You do look pale, at that."

"I'm fine, Dr. Gentry." I struggled to retain a facade of calmness. "It was not in your capacity as a doctor that I sent for you."

He had started to open his bag, but at my words he stared at me, then slowly reclosed it. I saw him shoot a glance at Marcus, who was merely looking puzzled.

"What is it, Miss Ames?" Marcus asked pleasantly. "How can we help you?"

Now that the moment was at hand, I found it almost impossible to begin. Oh, how much easier it would have been if I could have just held out the ring! I took a deep breath and began.

"I asked you here in your joint capacity as executors of Raven Winfield's estate." I glanced from one to the other. Dr. Gentry's expression was carefully noncommittal, while Marcus still wore a puzzled look. "As you know, I go by the name of Selina Ames, though I had never thought that it was my real name. I was reared by a man named Henry Ames, who told me he was my foster father. Since coming to Bittercreek, I have unearthed evidence that makes me certain he was actually my natural father and that Rose Winfield was my natural mother."

Dr. Gentry's expression didn't change, but Marcus's look turned to one of incredulity. There was a long silence before he asked politely, "And on just what evidence do you base this theory?"

Though I felt my cheeks burn at his tone, I explained how I had happened to come to Bittercreek and what I had learned from the *Bulletin* and told them about the fragments of information I had gotten from Henry Ames.

Dr. Gentry remarked slowly, "That's a lot to find out in just a few days."

"Also," I added, "until recently I had in my possession a ring that he had given me. It was seeing that same ring in Raven's portrait that caused me to faint yesterday."

At that, Marcus's incredulous expression faded and was replaced by something else, something to which I couldn't quite put a name.

"I see." His voice held an odd note. "Would you mind telling us where that ring is now?"

"I wish I knew," I answered. "It was stolen from this room while I was with you yesterday. I think it was taken to weaken my claim to Raven's Rise."

"Which it does, of course," Marcus said slowly. "Without the evidence of the ring, any claim of yours to be Rose Winfield's daughter is exceedingly nebulous."

CHAPTER SIX

I REALIZED THEN what I must have heard in his voice: skepticism, if not total disbelief. So much, I thought bitterly, for the flattery and pretty speeches.

Dr. Gentry cleared his throat. "Now wait a minute, Marcus," he said mildly. "I happen to know a couple of things that fit in with this young lady's story. Rose *was* pregnant when she left Bittercreek, and she *did* take Raven's emerald ring. Raven told me that last part of it herself, though she didn't know about the baby. And I didn't tell her. Seemed like she had enough to worry about as it was."

I was surprised and grateful for the doctor's support, but Marcus didn't seem to be affected by his words. "It is going to make no difference what fact either of us presents, Dr. Gentry," I said bluntly. "It is plain to see that Mr. Hannaford has decided that I am both a liar and an impostor."

Marcus's expression did change then, and he took an involuntary step toward me. "Not at all, Miss Ames. But what would you have me do? Raven Winfield entrusted everything she had to Doc Gentry's and my discretion. I am simply saying that we need clearcut proof before we can hand it over lock, stock and barrel to the first claimant, winsome though she may be. After all, you could have put this story together from what I had told you and the facts you got from the *Bulletin*. Even the letter from your 'benefactor' could have been written by you. Now, if he or she would come forward, or if you still had the ring—"

"You would probably find a reason to doubt that, too," I said. I couldn't keep the hurt and resentment out of my voice. "Either that it might be imitation or that I had stolen it from somewhere or that the portraits don't show it clearly enough—"

"No need to worry on that score," Dr. Gentry said gruffly. "I'd know that emerald of Raven's anywhere, even after all this time." He rubbed his face, considering me, then said to Marcus, "You know, Rose's hair was kind of red. Darker than hers, maybe, but still—"

"For Pete's sake, Doc!" For a moment Marcus's voice lost its charming, educated quality, and I caught a glimpse of the pragmatic saloonkeeper's son. "We'd be ridden out of town on a rail if we gave her Raven's Rise with no more to go on that what she's told us!" He turned again to me, and his voice had recovered its sophisticated overlay. "If you will just be patient, Miss Ames, it's possible that we can unearth some evidence that will back up your statements."

"Certainly," I said, equally as formal. "I am sure you will put forth great effort to that end. And you will continue to put it forth until the deadline for claiming the property will have passed." I stalked to the door and flung it open. "Thank you so much, gentlemen, and good day!"

I stood waiting for them to leave. Marcus was the first to move, and as he stopped before me, I saw to my fury that the amusement was back in his hazel eyes. He bowed low—an elaborate, overdone gesture. Then he smiled and said, "Another old wives' tale has been proven to be true. Redheads do have flaming tempers." Then he left hastily before I could think of a withering reply.

"Now calm down," Dr. Gentry ordered. "I'll work on him. In the meantime, do you have the slightest notion who took your ring?"

I told him briefly of my suspicions, which now sounded illogical to my own ears. "But there seems no reason why Mr. Soames should care all that much who inherits Raven's Rise," I finished. "Which is why I didn't mention it to you sooner."

"Hmm." The doctor looked thoughtful. He patted my arm. "You just sit tight and stop worrying. I'll talk to you later."

After he had gone, I succumbed to a fit of stormy weeping. I had been so sure that Marcus would believe me, that the two of us would have to convince Dr. Gentry that I was truly Raven's heir.

To my annoyance I realized that I was as disappointed at his attitude as I was at being denied my birthright. Which was ridiculous, because if I had Raven's fortune, any number of men might be attracted to me. Why, even in a town as small as this—

Jared Newcomb's arresting face flashed into my mind.

My crying spell came to a hiccuping stop. He had certainly seemed interested in me, though whether because he thought I was pretty or because he sensed a story for his newspaper, I didn't know. And at this moment I didn't care. I desperately needed someone to bolster my sagging ego.

Without stopping to consider my actions, I bathed my face and changed into my green-sprigged gown. Even though Mr. Marcus Hannaford didn't believe my story, Jared might. He would no doubt be delighted to report in his newspaper of the "winsome" claimant to the Winfield estate. But as I was ready to leave, I paused at the thought. Did I have anything to gain by that happening? The possibility of my benefactor's coming forward was most remote, for he or she obviously desired anonymity. And if Marcus chose not to believe me, then certainly the townspeople wouldn't be so inclined. Considering their self-interest in the matter, it could actually be dangerous. I decided not to seek out the newspaper editor, after all.

But I was far too restless to remain in my room. And as fate would have it, Jared was at the desk with Mr. Harper when I reached the lobby.

I would have gotten to the door without his noticing me, but when he caught the glance, half guilty, half resentful, that Mr. Harper sent in my direction, he turned to see who might be its recipient.

"Ah, Miss Ames!" he exclaimed. Those incredible blue eyes lit up with delight. "You are just the person I had hoped to see!" As he came toward me, I saw Mr. Harper give us a sullen glare before disappearing into a back room.

"What may I do for you, Mr. Newcomb?" I spoke somewhat warily, for I suspected him of having both an instinctive sense for newsworthy items and a powerful persuasive talent. And I remembered with dismay my promise to tell him about any important happening in my life.

Immediately, I realized that he had no intention of letting me forget it. He managed to convey a smiling reproach as he said, "A promise is a promise, Miss Ames. Rumor has it that a valuable piece of jewelry has been stolen from you, but I have yet to hear it from your lips. Might I offer you some refreshment in the dining room while you apprise me of the facts in the matter?"

"No, thank you," I returned. "Besides, if everyone in town already knows it, how can it be news?"

He fell in beside me as I walked to the door. "In this town everybody knows what is *said* to be going on. They buy the *Bulletin* to ascertain the actual facts of the matter." He held the door wide for me. "That's the way it is in this case. The story is that you are missing a valuable ring. Not only would I like to verify that, but my readers will be avid to know what kind of ring, its approximate value, whether or not it was an heirloom, whether you possibly mislaid it—as Mr. Harper contends—and whether or not you suspect anyone in particular of taking it." He was grinning now with a charming impertinence. I couldn't help returning his smile.

"Doesn't it occur to you or your readers that it might be none of their affair?" I spoke with mock severity.

"Of course not. If I thought that, I wouldn't be in this profession, and if they thought it, I would be out of business." He took my elbow as we stood together on the porch. "Might I ask where we are going?"

"I don't know your destination," I retorted, "but I am going for a walk." I started to move away from him, but at that instant I saw Marcus angling toward us from the saloon across the street. Swiftly, I added, "Of course, if you would care to accompany me—"

Jared hadn't missed my brief glance toward Marcus. He tucked my arm under his. "I'd be delighted. Even though—" his eyes sparkled with humor "—I am to be used as a foil in an affair of the heart."

There was no time to protest. Marcus had reached the boardwalk before the porch, and he paused politely. "Good afternoon, Miss Ames. Newcomb."

Jared murmured some response, and I nodded briefly. "Mr. Hannaford," I returned with noticeable coolness, and started past him.

Marcus's voice stopped me before I had gone two steps. "About that matter we spoke of earlier, Miss Ames. You would probably be wise not to discuss it with anyone just yet." For once his tone was serious, as was his glance at Jared.

"Secrets, Marcus?" Jared asked amiably. "Don't you know better than to hint of such things in my presence?"

I scarcely heard him for the indignation that was pouring through me. "Really, Mr. Hannaford," I remarked icily, "I am quite capable of handling my own affairs." With that I swept on down the boardwalk. It was a moment before Jared caught up with me.

"Well," he inquired mildly, "what was that all about?"

"I don't wish to discuss it," I answered stormily, "and if you try to do so, I shall continue my walk unaccompanied."

"Not a word," he said. For a time we marched silently side by side; then, as anger receded, my pace slowed. Soon we came to the end of the boardwalk, and I stopped, uncertain which direction to take. I glanced inquiringly at Jared. Eyes bright with humor, he shrugged and put one finger to his mouth in a sealed-lips gesture.

"Oh, for heaven's sake," I said crossly, "I didn't mean that you couldn't say *anything*." His attitude was making me feel I had been unbelievably childish. "I give you permission to point out a pleasant place to walk."

"Certainly. Just ahead is Bitter Creek, for which the town is named. A path at the side of the bridge leads to a shaded area close to the water. It is always cooler there."

"That sounds nice." All at once I felt overwarm and very tired. "Will you take me there, Mr. Newcomb?"

"Of course. But will you call me Jared? I'd like to think we are friends."

Friends. I had thought Marcus might become my friend. Was that why I felt this aching sensation in the region of my heart?

Jared didn't press me for an answer, for which I was grateful, and soon we came to the path he had mentioned. The swiftly flowing creek was just below us, and as we reached the trees that shaded it, I felt a delightful coolness. With a sigh I sat on one of the smooth, flat stones that conveniently dotted the bank.

"I wish you *would* let me be your friend," Jared remarked quietly. "That sigh sounded as though you could use one."

I said bleakly, "How does one recognize a true friend? You are no doubt hoping for a story for the *Bulletin*, while Marcus—"

"Don't underestimate Marcus, Selina. While he isn't overfond of me, I, on the other hand, admire him greatly. You could do worse than to rely on his judgment, whatever the matter."

I felt my eyes fill. "I can't rely on him at all! How can I, when he won't even believe me? And without the ring—" I broke off abruptly.

Interest flared in his eyes; then he shook his black mane of hair. "No, I won't pry. It is obviously of great importance. No doubt Marcus was right when he told you not to speak of it."

At his words the hurt and anger came surging back. "I don't see why I shouldn't speak of it. He and Dr. Gentry are never going to give me what is rightfully mine, anyhow, without the ring."

He sat very still, watching me.

"The emerald ring," I heard myself amending. "The one Raven is wearing in her portraits."

And then for the third time that day I found myself pouring out the story of my life and of my coming to Bittercreek, this time in much greater detail. I knew that I should not, knew that I would be sorry, but somehow I couldn't stop the torrent of words.

"So you are Raven Winfield's granddaughter," he said when I had at last fallen silent.

"If you choose to believe it. Certainly none of your readers will do me that kindness." I was already regretting my outburst.

"Don't worry about that. I do believe you, but not a word of this will be printed in the *Bulletin* until you have been officially accepted as Raven's heir. It wouldn't be safe. And I want no harm to come to you because of me."

Gratitude welled up in me. "Thank you, Jared," I said. "Perhaps I really do have a friend, after all."

THAT EVENING, after a solitary dinner, I went again to Raven's Rise. As I stood on the boardwalk before it, its dark mass loomed over me as before, yet there was a difference, for now I knew that we were linked irrevocably. Though Rose had never lived there, her blood ran in my veins, and through her, my grandmother's blood. I could feel that blood now, racing, coursing through me. I wanted to walk up the steps and enter the wide entry hall, go into the library with its book-lined walls, drift silently through the maze of endless corridors.

I didn't realize I had moved at all until the cool metal of the iron gate touched my palms. I felt as though shaken abruptly from a dream, a dream so vivid that it was hard to tell which was the fantasy and which reality. I leaned my forehead against the bars and bit my lips to stem the bitter longing.

Some whisper of sound caused me to whirl quickly around, and a scream froze in my throat as I saw the figure standing not far behind me. He was a giant of a man, and he was as black as the shadows in which he stood. The pale light from a sliver of moon caught a shine of metal, and I realized that a shotgun dangled from one huge hand.

The servant, Hiram.

Even through the terror that seized me, I was immediately aware of his identity. A flood of relief unlocked my vocal cords.

"How dare you sneak up and startle me like that!" I burst out. Shock made my voice sharp with anger.

He moved menacingly toward me. "What for you hangin' 'round Miss Raven's property?" Though his voice was uneducated and spoke of the Deep South, there was none of the black man's humility in his tone. "Ain't nobody can touch Miss Raven's property without her say-so."

I stood my ground. "This is a public walkway." I was still trembling violently, but I didn't mean for him to know it. "Besides, Miss Winfield is dead."

"Well, she done give orders in her will, and till Mr. Marcus and the doc tells me different, I'm takin' care of her place like always."

His loyalty was admirable, but I was still too shaken to care. "That may be," I persisted stubbornly, "but I have the right to stand here and admire it if I choose." I glanced once more at the great, dark mansion and caught my breath sharply. "Besides, you are hardly doing your duty at the moment. I think someone is in the library. I see a tiny light moving about in there."

He gave a startled exclamation and came to peer over my shoulder. Then, with a muffled oath, he ran forward, put a hand on the brick gatepost and vaulted over. In a second he had disappeared into the dark bulk of shrubbery at the side of the house. I lingered a long time, but I heard no sounds, saw no more lights. At last, reluctantly, I went back to the hotel.

As I climbed the stairs to my room, I realized that I was bone-weary, undoubtedly from the emotional unheavals of the day. I had discovered my identity, I had been within reach of my birthright and been denied it; I had been on the threshold of falling in love. I didn't even bother to light the lamp but disrobed by the pale square of light from the window, then put on my nightgown and crept into bed. In spite of the turbulence of the day, I fell almost instantly to sleep.

It wasn't until the next morning that I discovered my emerald ring. It lay on the oaken washstand, precisely where I had left it.

CHAPTER SEVEN

I HAD THOUGHT I knew why the ring was stolen. I had no idea why it had been returned. I wasn't foolish enough to believe that my threat of going to the authorities had influenced Mr. Soames, if, indeed, it had been he who had instigated the theft. And while Mr. Harper had obviously been disturbed by it, I doubted that his feelings in the matter carried much weight. I only knew that with the emerald once more nestled in its velvet pouch in my pocketbook, it was as though a great weight had been removed from my heart. Marcus would have to believe me now; Dr. Gentry had stated flatly that he would be able to identify the ring beyond doubt.

I dressed quickly and went downstairs. Where might I find the doctor and Marcus this time of day? Quite possibly the hotel dining room, I decided, and though this immediately proved to be untrue, the fragrant odors eminating from the kitchen reminded me that I was inordinately hungry. I hesitated, torn between healthy appetite and the overwhelming desire to vindicate myself to Marcus. Before I could decide which need was uppermost, Jared Newcomb came into the dining room from the street door. He looked pleased when he saw me and came over immediately.

"Selina! Is it possible that by some good fortune you haven't as yet broken your fast? And that, if so, you might be inveigled into joining me?"

His geniality always amused me, and it did so especially this morning, when my mood was equally light.

"You are right on both counts, kind sir," I answered. "I would be delighted to join you."

He seated me at a nearby table, then, as he took the other chair, said, "Do I detect a rather more cheerful aspect this morning? I hardly dare think that happy smile stems solely from my presence."

I gave him a teasing glance over the menu Ellie presented. Oh, how good it felt to be with someone with whom I didn't have to be on guard! "That is a part of it, certainly, but—" I let him wait while we gave our breakfast orders.

"But what?" he demanded after Ellie had gone. "Have you discovered some other facts to help you? Or—" his eyes widened, and the heavy black brows rose to new heights "—has the missing evidence been returned?"

"It has," I confessed. "Why, I don't know, but it was there, just where I had left it the day before. Don't you see what this means, Jared?" In the telling, it became real to me at last, and I felt ready to burst with excitement. "It means—" I lowered my voice to a whisper. "It means that Raven's Rise is actually mine! Mine! No doubt I can move in tomorrow if I wish!"

He sat back in his chair as though overwhelmed by my disclosure. "That is wonderful news, Selina. I really am happy for you. But surely you don't intend to live there!"

"Why—whyever not?" I hadn't even considered any other course.

"Wouldn't you be lonely? It is so large, and there seems so much unhappiness connected to it." He leaned forward and put his hand over mine. "As Miss Winfield's heir, you will inherit more than Raven's Rise. There is surely a goodly sum of money, also. Why don't you consider putting the house up for sale? Much as Bittercreek and I would miss you, I feel that in the city you would have a greater chance of happiness."

Slowly, I pulled my hand from beneath his. "If by 'city' you mean San Francisco, there is nothing for me there." I thought briefly of my foster mother and her implacable hatred. "Why shouldn't I make Bittercreek my home? You seem to like it well enough."

He shrugged. "I stay because it gives me the illusion of independence. But Bittercreek is not a friendly town. There seems to be something—some malaise of spirit—that keeps its citizens distrustful and suspicious, and Raven's Rise is a part of it." He shook his head, and one black lock fell over the broad forehead. "Believe me, Selina, you wouldn't be happy here."

Ellie brought our orders, and I said no more until she had gone. Though he had not lessened my determination to live in the mansion, I was crestfallen and hurt at his attitude.

Jared must have seen my distress. "Forgive me, Selina. I didn't mean to upset you or to ruin your meal.

Go on with it, please. After all, nothing must be decided right away."

He was right, of course. Marcus might even yet refuse to accept the ring as proof. But I didn't really believe that, and at the thought of confronting him with it, my good spirits returned. I picked up my knife and fork with renewed interest. Jared, however, barely touched his food, and seeking to placate him, I leaned across the table and whispered conspiratorially, "Cheer up, Jared. As soon as this is settled, you can print the story. And think of the number of newspapers you will sell when word gets out!"

He smiled, but it didn't completely erase the troubled look in his eyes.

I DIDN'T FIND Dr. Gentry at his office, nor did I see Marcus anywhere on the street. As I wouldn't seek him out at his saloon, I had to content myself with dispatching a note there and returning to wait in my hotel room.

It wasn't long, however, before Marcus appeared at my door; to my mixed dismay and delight, he was alone.

"Doc Gentry is out on a call," he told me. "If you would rather I come again when he gets back—"

"No, not at all," I answered hastily. My stomach was fluttering nervously, and I felt that a protracted postponement would be my undoing. I swung the door wider. "Please, come in."

When I ignored the proprieties and closed the door behind him, he regarded me quizzically. "Are you sure that you should do that? There is apt to be gossip—"

"Oh, bother the gossip!" I said impatiently. "I have something to show you, and I simply cannot wait any longer." I got the velvet pouch from my pocketbook, opened it and withdrew the emerald ring. "Here," I said, and held it out to him. "This is proof of my claim to Raven's Rise. If that doesn't satify you and Dr. Gentry, then nothing will."

He stared at it, then lifted his eyes to mine. "How did you get it back?"

"Someone's guilty conscience, I suppose. But for whatever reason, it has been returned. Now do you believe that I am Raven Winfield's granddaughter?"

He took the ring from my hand and gazed at it for a long moment. At last, he said prosaically, "It looks to be genuine, and it certainly resembles the ring in her portraits. When considered along with the other facts you have given us, it appears that you actually are the heir to the Winfield estate. It will, of course, be some time before the legalities have—"

"I would like to move in tomorrow," I said firmly.

Dismay touched his handsome features. "You would actually move into Raven's Rise? You plan to live there? Alone?"

"My grandmother did," I pointed out. "For some seventeen years. And except for the servants, she was quite alone."

"Yes, and why she chose to do it, I'll never understand!" His voice took on a passion that surprised me. "She was still beautiful, still desirable, still in the very prime of life, yet she chose to shut herself up in that mausoleum with her memories and her lost dreams and her dust-covered baubles!" He came close to me.

"But at least she had lived, Selina! She had known love and triumph and the joy of a child. Why would an attractive young woman like yourself want to take up residence in that haunted house?"

I was trembling with outrage and something more—some icy fear with which his words had touched me. "Because it is mine!" I stormed with a passion that more than matched his. "Can't you understand that? Can't any of you understand? Do you know what it is to grow up owning nothing, possessing nothing except what is grudgingly lent you—even including your name? Do you know how it feels to be constantly reminded that the very clothes you stand in are yours only by the grace of someone's charity? Well, I do, but not anymore! Raven's Rise and all that goes with it are mine, and I want the world to know it!"

"Poor little girl," Marcus said, and the compassion in his voice nearly undid me. He came to me and took me in his arms. "Poor lonely, lost little girl."

I hadn't known I was crying until he began to kiss the tears away.

I DID NOT MOVE IN the next day, but before many days had passed, the legal technicalities had been ironed out, and I was free to take possession of Raven's Rise.

My most immediate concern was with regard to the servants, Dulcie and Hiram. Would they welcome me as a relative of their beloved mistress, or would they resent me as an interloper? My brief encounters with each of them had not been reassuring.

Marcus had explained that I was not duty-bound to retain them if I didn't wish to do so. "Miss Winfield

left them a generous annuity, so that if they are careful, they needn't work at all. However, they came here
from the South with her, and I doubt that they have
ties anywhere else.''

I hadn't known that my grandmother came from the
South and stored the information away for future
consideration. ''I think that I will have to talk to them
before I can decide,'' I told him. ''As much as anything, it is how they feel about me.''

SO IT WAS that trepidation was mixed with the tremulous excitement I felt when at last we stood on the walk
before the mansion and Marcus presented me with the
keys to my inheritance.

''I am happy for you, Selina,'' he said, ''and even
happier for Raven, for I know she would want you to
have it. But she didn't possess this house; it possessed
her. Try not to let that happen to you.''

I scarcely heard him. My hand was shaking as I took
the heavy ring of keys. He had singled out an ornate
brass one for me. I was almost in a daze as I approached the wide, paneled front door with it. Just as
I was about to fit the key into the lock, the door swung
inward, and Dulcie stood there, regarding me dispas-
sionately. I fought a keen disappointment.

Her eyes briefly touched the key in my hand, then
returned to mine. ''Sorry,'' she said, ''but Miss Raven
didn't like to bother with that. I usually opened the
door for her. Welcome home, Miss Selina.''

My disappointment vanished. ''Thank you, Dulcie.'' I turned to Marcus, who had followed me onto
the porch. ''Won't you come in, Mr. Hannaford?''

"If you will forgive me, I have some urgent business to attend to. Perhaps later?"

We spoke as though that time when he had kissed away my tears had never been. Indeed, we had not again alluded to it, but I had been aware ever since of a subtle electricity that ran between us. I knew it only awaited the right circumstance for me to be drawn back to his arms as though by a magnet.

"Of course. Might I expect you for dinner?" I deliberately refrained from glancing at Dulcie. Surely the mistress of a home like this need not consult her housekeeper before inviting guests.

Marcus bowed slightly. "I would be honored." Our eyes met and held, and I knew that he, too, felt the electricity. "Until this evening, then."

When his tall, graceful figure had passed through the iron gate, I turned back to the open door. I no longer noticed Dulcie, who stood silently to one side. I took a deep breath. This was the moment I had longed for, had dreamed of, had thought would never really happen. Despite my stirrings of love for Marcus, I was glad that he was gone, for I wanted it all to myself.

Once again I stepped into the spacious entry hall with its polished floor. Again I felt that air of quiet waiting. I walked slowly to the narrow hall table and gazed at my reflection in the mirror that hung over it. The girl who returned my look was the same one I had seen in my glass at the hotel this morning—clear green eyes beneath a mass of flaming hair, slightly turned up nose with its dusting of tiny freckles, rounded chin with just a hint of a cleft—yet I also seemed to see another image, this one with black wings of hair and large, dark eyes that glowed with love and pride and passion.

"Can I get you some tea, Miss Selina?" Dulcie's voice seemed to come from a great distance.

Dazedly, I turned to her. "What? What did you say?" I murmured.

She was looking at me rather oddly. "I asked if I could serve you some tea. Miss Raven usually had it in the library. It was her favorite room."

"Why—yes, I would like that, Dulcie." I undid the strings of my bonnet, and she took it from me. "But first I want to explore the house a little. I haven't really seen it yet, you know."

After hanging up my bonnet, I started down the hall toward the back of the house, bypassing the parlor and library, which I had already seen. Behind the parlor was the dining room with its long polished table that could easily seat twelve. A massive crystal chandelier hung over it. Against one wall stood a huge carved breakfront of truly fabulous beauty that was filled with delicate china. Who had sat with her at that table, I wondered. Had the chairs ever held laughing, chattering people, or had she dined each night in solitary splendor and filled the places with ghosts of what might have been?

I closed the sliding pocket doors and crossed the hall. It was apparently the drawing room I entered next. Its furniture was stiff and formal, and scattered among the heavier pieces were several smaller chairs that were covered with slippery satin. An enormous grand piano stood in one corner near the window, a

piece of music still open on its stand. Over the fireplace mantel hung a portrait, not as well done as the
others but immensely appealing, of a young girl
swiftly approaching womanhood. She was holding a
rose, and the painter had caught not only a tremulous
beauty in the eyes and the dark russet mane that hung
over one shoulder but also an air of self-satisfaction
in the smile. I realized with a start that it no doubt was
a portrait of my mother.

Behind the dining room were the kitchen and pan-
try and another door that probably led to the servants' quarters. Next to the drawing room was what
seemed to be a ladies' powder closet, and another door
led to a steep, narrow stairway that I took to be the
maid's stair.

I had meant to explore the upper floors, but when I
returned to the front stairs, I felt surprisingly tired. I
had not slept well the night before, in anticipation of
this day, and I supposed that accounted for it. I went,
instead, into the library, whose quiet dignity appealed
to me as it had before. I passed the comfortable chairs
and couch and went directly to the portrait of Raven
that hung over the mantel. As I gazed at her, she regarded me with her enigmatic smile, and I felt a sudden, warm satisfaction. She wanted me here—I was
sure of it—and I was pleased to think that I had
brought her a modicum of happiness at last.

I heard a sound and turned to find Dulcie coming
in with the tea tray. Hiram was with her, but he hesitated in the doorway. Something in his attitude re-

minded me of a dog my foster family had once owned, who, when scolded, had hesitated to come into the light and warmth of the kitchen without a specific invitation.

Dulcie set the tray on a nearby table and jerked a nod over her shoulder at him. "It's Hiram," she said unnecessarily. "He doesn't know whether he's welcome or not."

"Come in, Hiram," I said. "Why don't you think you are welcome?"

Though there was humility in his attitude as his great bulk stood before me, there was none in his reply.

"Why for didn't you tell me you was Miss Raven's kin?" he demanded. "I wouldn't of talked so smart-like had I knowed."

"I realize that," I said. "You were just looking after Miss Raven's interests. I didn't tell you she was my grandmother because I didn't think you would believe me."

He scrutinized me carefully. "Mebbe I wouldn't of. But now I knows, I can see you favor her some."

Though this was mostly wishful thinking on Hiram's part, I realized that it was a high compliment and decided to press my advantage.

"Would you like to work for me, Hiram, you and Dulcie? Just as you did for Miss Raven?" Though I didn't show it outwardly, I awaited his answer with some apprehension. The story of my inheriting Raven's Rise had not yet come out in the newspaper, but there were bound to be repercussions of some sort when it did. I would feel much more comfortable if he and Dulcie were still in residence.

"Can't never be the same," Hiram said almost truculently. "She brung us out from slavery and give us our papers long time afore Mr. Lincoln did. She and we was family." He thought a moment. "But I reckon we'll stick around a spell, seein' as how you're supposed to be her kin."

Supposed to be. Then there was still a doubt between them. I decided not to remark on it. "And you, Dulcie?"

"Hiram is my man," she said. "He decides what we'll do."

I hid my surprise. She seemed so much more educated than Hiram that I would have thought she was the decision maker.

"Then it's settled," I said. "Now may I have my tea?"

Dulcie served me, then followed Hiram out of the room. As I sat in one of the fireplace chairs and sipped the steaming beverage, I regarded my surroundings with a consuming interest. This was Raven's favorite room, Dulcie had said. She had doubtless spent long hours here, dreaming by the fire, reading the many books that lined its walls.

Setting down my cup, I rose and went to examine them. From early childhood I had always loved books; they had been my one escape from the cold realities of my life. I had cherished those few that had been allowed me, and I was happy to think that I shared that love with my grandmother. But to my disappointment, most of the books looked as though they had never been read. I discovered, as I took one after the other from its place, that in many the pages remained uncut. Entire shelves of volumes were matching sets, bought, I surmised, because of their handsome exteriors rather than their content, and I didn't recognize the names or authors of any of them.

I turned my back to the wall of books and surveyed the room. How, then, had Raven filled the many hours she must have spent here? Did she do handiwork, write letters or simply sit and dream of her dead love and lost child? I realized sharply just how little I really knew of this woman with whom I identified so strongly.

And yet I felt her presence even now.

My eye fell on the large leather-topped desk that stood in the front bay window. Perhaps it contained papers that would tell me more about her. Perhaps— my heart quickened—she had even kept a journal.

To my surprise the desk drawers were locked. I started for the bellpull to summon Dulcie, then paused in mid-stride. Of course. The key to the desk would be among those Marcus had given me. I got the large brass ring from my pocketbook, which I had brought with me into the library. There were, indeed, two tiny keys that looked as though they might fit the miniature locks. To my delight, the first one I tried fit exactly.

Eagerly, I explored the contents of each drawer. To my disappointment, I found very little that would add to my knowledge of my grandmother. The drawers were very neat and contained only those things that any desk might have—pens, an inkpot, a quantity of good-quality notepaper and envelopes. A packet of letters appeared to be only about business concerns. There was a ledger whose entries were written in the flowing style of an educated woman, but they were cryptic and had no meaning to me. In not one of the drawers was there a scrap of personal correspondence, nor was there the journal I had hoped to find.

I went again to stand before her portrait. The dark eyes that smiled into mine gave no hint of loneliness or sorrow, and it occurred to me that the picture had to have been painted long before this house was built, and even before my mother had disappeared, for in it Raven wore the emerald ring that Rose had taken with her.

Dulcie came in just then to take the tea things. Without turning around, I asked, "Where was this portrait painted, Dulcie? Not here in Bittercreek, surely."

She stood beside me. "That one and the one in the parlor are from when she was still married to Miss Rose's daddy, and Miss Raven brought 'em west with us. That was about all she did bring, too. Most all she had when she died she got by outworking and outthinking everybody else."

I had never considered that once I must have also had a grandfather. "What became of him—Rose's father? And how did my grandmother happen to come to California?"

"He was shot in a duel—over her." Dulcie shook the black-turbaned head. "It wasn't none of her doing. Men just naturally lost their heads when it came to her. But his family couldn't forgive her for it—no more than they could forgive her for not being a proper widow woman and hiding behind a veil for the rest of her life. So she loaded up a wagon with Hiram and me and Miss Rose and those pictures, and we started out west, where the gold was." Her voice grew husky as she added, "She didn't have much for a time, but however little it was, she shared it with Hiram and me."

I looked at the portrait with new respect and a subtle sense of shame. I had had only myself to worry about; she had been burdened with three others who depended on her.

"Did she never correspond with her husband's family? They were Rose's relatives, after all."

Dulcie shook her head. "If she did, I never knew it. But there might be something in her bedroom desk. She did all of her personal letter writing up there."

"She did?" I felt a surge of excitement. That might be a more logical place to keep a journal. "Where is it? Have you put my things in there?"

I could see the shock that Dulcie experienced at my words. "Why, no, I—" She caught herself and spoke with quiet dignity. "It wouldn't be right for anyone but Miss Raven to have that room."

I could see how it might seem that way to her. "I understand," I said. "I would like to see it now, however."

I sensed her relief. "It's at the front of the house. The middle room, just above the stairs."

I took my pocketbook and keys and hurried upstairs. The central door stood ajar. I pushed it open and went in.

I scarcely noticed the silk-draped four-poster bed or the wardrobe that stretched half the length of the room. My eyes were drawn immediately to the dainty escritoire that stood, as did the desk in the library, in the large bay window. But this faced away from the room, toward the vista that could be seen through the transparent curtains. I went over and sat in the straight chair that had been placed before it. In front of me lay the entire town, spread out with the clarity of a child's toy village beneath a Christmas tree. I could see a dog ambling across the street, three youngsters playing marbles in the dust, and even as I watched, Dr. Gentry came out of his office and strolled in the direction of the Red Garter saloon.

From this vantage point, I realized with an odd chill of discovery, Raven Winfield had been privy to the movements, the whereabouts, the comings and goings, of every man, woman and child in Bittercreek.

CHAPTER EIGHT

IT WAS IMMEDIATELY APPARENT to me that the house had been arranged with this in mind, just as it had no doubt been built as a constant reminder of Raven Winfield's presence in Bittercreek. What I didn't understand was why she had felt the need for it. It seemed inconsistent with the mental image I had of her.

On the desk's surface were a plumed pen protruding from a gold inkstand whose contents had gone dry, a curved blotter and a small oval daguerreotype. This last I picked up and examined. It was the likeness of a young man with dark, carefully parted hair and handsome handlebar mustache. He was very attractive, and even the rigors of posing for the photographer hadn't dimmed the twinkle in his eyes. I concluded from his soft collar and the bandanna tie he wore that he was a Westerner and undoubtedly the murdered miner the newspaper had linked with Raven. Compassion touched me at the thought of her keeping his portrait on her desk for all these years.

I was about to try the drawers when Dulcie appeared in the open door.

"You have a caller," she said, and I thought I heard a hint of disapproval. "Mr. Newcomb of the newspaper is here to see you."

"So soon?" I asked, but I was pleased. "Show him into the library, will you?"

The disapproval became more apparent. "Miss Raven always saw such as him in the parlor."

I paused in the act of checking my appearance in Raven's mirror. "Such as him? Dulcie, Mr. Newcomb is my friend."

The cat's eyes narrowed, but she forebore to comment further. Feeling obscurely guilty, I added, "It is just that the parlor seems so awfully crowded."

"That's the way Miss Raven liked it," she said, and I sensed that this was the ultimate argument. "Those were all her favorite things. She wouldn't even let me dust in there, but took care of it herself."

"And so will I, if you like," I said. "But for this afternoon, Dulcie, the library, please." I went on tidying my hair before the glass and pretended not to see the tightened lips. After a moment she vanished, and I waited a little before following her down the stairs. Much as I admired and felt a decided rapport with my grandmother, I didn't intend to let Dulcie force me into her mold.

When I entered the library, Jared was standing, hands clasped behind his back, before Raven's portrait. He glanced at me as I came to stand beside him.

"So this is the famous painting and the equally famous emerald ring," he said by way of greeting.

"Yes. Isn't she beautiful?"

"Very beautiful and very elegant. But I happen to admire a more earthy type—say, with red hair and freckles."

"And you call yourself a friend!" I answered in mock annoyance. "No friend would ever notice a lady's freckles!"

"It is a part of my craft to notice things. For instance—" he reached for my left hand and lifted it "—I noticed at once that you are again wearing this."

The huge emerald glittered in its circlet of diamonds. "I'm afraid not to, after its disappearance," I said. "It has really become something of a burden."

He turned my hand so that the ring caught the light from a nearby window. "There are those who would be happy to relieve you of that burden."

"I know. If I trusted Mr. Soames, I'd have him lock it up in his bank vault, but that would be like asking a wolf to tend my sheep."

The blue eyes lit with laughter. "You still suspect him, then, of purloining it?"

"I do. But it scarcely matters now. I have Raven's Rise." I was afraid I said it more smugly than I meant to.

"Ah, yes. And the whole of Bittercreek knows it, down to the last exciting detail." He picked up a newspaper from the nearby table and held it out to me. "Here is your copy. You might want to keep it for your grandchildren."

I didn't take it. "And the details include the fact that I am illegitimate?"

He let the paper drop to his side, then laid it carefully on the table again. "There was no way to tell the story without that, Selina. It cannot be held against you."

I almost smiled at his naïveté. "It can and will. But I suppose it doesn't matter." I glanced again at Raven's portrait. "She was a saloonkeeper, yet this town respected her."

His silence was so pointed that I turned to look at him.

"They feared her," he said slowly. "It sometimes amounts to the same thing."

I thought of the view from the upstairs window, and a tremor ran through me. "Why?" I demanded. "Why should they fear her? Because she had money? I have heard there are others in this town richer than she. Banker Soames, for instance, or Mayor— Mayor—"

"Ogilvey," Jared supplied. "That's true; there are several. But nevertheless, they feared her. I have often wondered why."

The sensation that overcame me had more than anger in it. "I'm surprised you haven't ferreted out some reason or other by now," I said coldly. "And it isn't yet too late. I suppose it is even acceptable to malign a dead woman if it will sell newspapers."

Concern leaped into his eyes. "Have I offended you? Selina, I'm sorry! I didn't—" He abruptly stopped speaking, and I saw that Dulcie had come to the open door.

"Sorry to interrupt," she said, though she didn't sound sorry. "I just wanted to check with you about dinner. Mr. Marcus's favorite is ham and candied yams.'' She slanted a glance at Jared, and I knew she had mentioned Marcus quite deliberately.

"It's all right, Dulcie," I said. "Mr. Newcomb was just leaving."

"Yes," Jared said. "That might be best." He started toward the door, then paused and said softly, "I wish I knew what you are afraid of."

I didn't answer, and he went out, with Dulcie right behind him. For a long moment I considered again the painting of my lovely grandmother. I wish I knew, too, I thought uneasily.

WHEN I RETURNED UPSTAIRS I didn't go into Raven's bedroom, but went instead to the one next to it, where Dulcie had put my belongings. It was as though I had no wish to view again that startling vista or to contemplate its possible meaning.

My small trunk stood empty; Dulcie had already put away its contents. My bed was a high four-poster similar to that in Raven's room. Its thick feather mattress must have been recently plumped up, for its height necessitated the set of wooden steps that stood beside it. I viewed them with some amusement. Falling out of bed would be disastrous, I decided.

My amusement faded as I considered my meager wardrobe. Now I could have any number of new gowns, for though I had not yet had a complete accounting of the assets of my estate, Marcus had assured me that there was ready cash for any conceivable need that should arise. But I had not yet had time to take advantage of it, and my immediate concern was what I should wear to dinner with him. He had seen the prettiest of my gowns, and like any young woman on the fringes of romance, I wanted to dazzle him with something exciting and new.

I thought of the huge wardrobe in Raven's room, then dismissed it. Despite her beauty, she must have been nearing sixty when she died and doubtless would have taken to wearing a totally different type of attire from that in the portraits. Had she, I wondered, grown gray and stout? The thought saddened me, and I realized that I visualized her always as the slim, young figure in the paintings. Perhaps, I thought, I wouldn't find her story so appealing if it were not for that.

I had at last chosen the green challis gown, which Dulcie had freshened and pressed, and the glow of approval in Marcus's eyes had compensated me for the lack of a new one. He looked even more handsome than usual as we sat across from each other at the wide dining-room table, and I was bemused by the way the light from the chandelier caught and held in the chestnut highlights of his dark hair. It must have been as kind to me, for he suddenly said, "Under this light, Selina, your hair has the look of burnished gold! You are as beautiful as your grandmother ever was."

Having perfectly good eyesight, I accepted this for the gentlemanly elaboration that it was, but it gave me the opportunity to ask, "What did she look like in her later years? Had she changed a great deal, do you think?"

He set down his wineglass. "That was one of the incredible things about her. She wasn't young when I first knew her, possibly thirty-five or more, but she

was even more lovely than she looked in those portraits. And later, even after tragedy had befallen her,
she retained her beauty of face and form.'' He took
another sip of wine and then added, as though com-
pelled, ''But she didn't have the gentle serenity of the
woman in those paintings, Selina. She had an air of
implacability, of iron determination, that sometimes
made one a little uneasy in her presence.''

Once again I leaped to her defense. ''I consider that
quite understandable,'' I said. ''She had lost both her
daughter and the man she loved. She is to be com-
mended for not allowing her bitterness to destroy her.''

''Didn't she? She turned her back on any future
happiness. Doc Gentry loved her; my father loved her.
There were probably many others, for though the few
women of the town disapproved of her, men admired
and respected her. But after Will Prentiss's death, she
never looked at another.''

I gazed at him—the hazel eyes that held no laughter now, the thick, tangled lashes, the chestnut lock
that had sprung into curl at his temple. ''Perhaps,'' I
said, and looked down at my plate, ''some men are
irreplaceable.''

There was an extended silence, but I didn't dare
look up. At last, he said, ''I am beginning to suspect
that is true of some women, also.''

I did look up then. The smile had returned to his
eyes, but he was no longer laughing at me. I felt a de-
liciously nervous flutter begin at the base of my throat,
and had not the table been between us, I would have
gone without hesitation into his arms.

"I don't suppose anyone cares that there's pecan pie for dessert," Dulcie said practically. I hadn't even been aware that she had enterd the room. I could feel a blush warm my cheeks, but Marcus only gave her a conspiratorial smile.

"Not just now," he said, and rising, put out a hand to me. I took it as though mesmerized. "If Miss Ames does not object, we will have coffee later, in the library. Much later, Dulcie."

Without so much as a backward glance, we floated—I floated, at any rate—across the hall and to the library. There, beneath my grandmother's gaze, I went eagerly into his arms.

I WAS STILL FLOATING or so it seemed, when at last he had gone and I took a candle and went upstairs. We had kissed and we had talked, as lovers will, about everything—and about nothing. It was enough for me just now that I had had opportunity at last to run my fingers through those crisp dark curls, to trace the arching brows, to melt with delightful weakness as his soft, tender lips captured mine. Time enough to talk of the future. I was rich, I was beautiful—he had persuaded me of it at last—and I was in love. I could scarcely ask for more.

And yet some compulsion stopped me before the door to my grandmother's room, perhaps because my happiness brought a deepened awareness of her solitude. Once again I wanted to know her, to understand her, as though by so doing I could even yet ease the pain she must have suffered.

My eyes again fell upon her desk, behind which the shades had been drawn to hide the view that troubled me. Impulsively, I crossed to it, and setting my candlestick down, pulled open the center drawer to reveal a leather-bound book that looked very much like the journal I had so hoped to find. I eagerly took it out and placed it on the desktop and, scarcely aware of my actions, sat down and pulled the candle closer.

The moment I opened the book, I knew that I was again to be disappointed, for it was simply an appointment book filled with brief notations in that same flowing feminine hand. The dates were of the previous year, and as I rifled through it, I noticed that the notations stopped abruptly near its end. The last entry, December tenth, was "Ogilvey," and the hour, five o'clock. I wondered if the mayor had been the last to see her, except for the servants.

The book also revealed that her life had not been as solitary as I had envisioned it. There were frequent visitors to tea, and she had held an occasional dinner party whose guests were neatly listed. I saw Marcus's name and Dr. Gentry's and often and at regular intervals those of Mr. Soames and Mayor Ogilvey. There was also, periodically, that of Senator Bentley. The occasional woman who called was invariably accompanied by her husband, and I remembered that first Jared and then Marcus had spoken of the disapproval of the townswomen. In the light of their antipathy, I wondered that they had come at all.

The candle flickered softly as I leafed through the book's pages. Other than Dr. Gentry, Soames and Ogilvey seemed to have been the most faithful, for they came almost invariably on the first and fifteenth of each month, unless it fell on Sunday, and always at the hour of five o'clock. It was surprising, I mused idly, that they and she had become such fast friends, considering that she had once accused them of murder.

At the thought, I straightened in my chair. Just how *had* this camaraderie come about, and when? She must have learned that she had been mistaken and acknowledged it, but even so, it took men of large and generous spirit to forgive having been publicly accused of such a heinous crime. I would not have thought it possible of Mr. Soames. Either he had swallowed his resentment toward Raven because of her significant business dealings with his bank, or there was something else he had had to gain.

Or something he had to lose.

I searched the remaining desk drawers, but the appointment books for the past years were not there. Neither were they in the dresser or the highboy. I thought a moment. If she had, indeed, saved them, they might possibly be on one of the library shelves.

I took the candle and went back to the stairway. It was only then, as I started down the long flight of stairs, that I became aware of the utter darkness. Dulcie and Hiram, thinking that I had retired, must have gone to bed also, for there wasn't the faintest trace of light anywhere, nor could I hear a sound beyond that of my own breathing. There came unbidden to my mind the memory of that tiny firefly of light I had seen on two occasions and of Hiram's face as he had leapt the gate and gone after it.

It was then that I heard my name spoken in a soft, drawn-out whisper.

"Selina—"

My heart jerked wildly in my breast. The whisper seemed to float toward me from the dark regions below.

"Who—" I tried to say, but scarcely a sound got past my quivering lips.

"Selina—" It came again, with that drawn-out sibilance that stirred the hair upon my nape. I clutched the banister, and my candle shook so violently its flame almost went out. At that moment I caught a subtle perfume that seemed to waft up the stairway toward me, an essence of faded things, of drying petals, of precious memories long packed and sadly stored away.

Attar of roses.

"Grandmother?" I breathed. "Grandmother, is it you?"

Again I caught the scent, again the sibilant whisper of my name.

"Selina—"

It was a sound so sad, so lonely, so utterly beseeching, that I found myself drawn toward it, drawn down the stairs into that total darkness.

My foot caught on a tred, and the tilted candle dropped hot wax onto my hand. I screamed aloud. And once started, I could not stop, but sent shriek echoing after shriek through the empty mansion.

CHAPTER NINE

I NEVER KNEW where Hiram came bursting from, or Dulcie, either, for that matter. But dimly, beneath my hysterical screaming, I heard a door slam open, then the heavy pounding of Hiram's tread as he rushed up the stairs to me.

"My land, Miss Selina, what done happened?" As he spoke, he took my candlestick from me and set it on the stair. I couldn't speak, but only shrank there, weeping.

Dulcie peered over his shoulder. "Is she hurt, Hiram? Quick, bring her downstairs and fetch Doc Gentry!"

"No! Not downstairs!" I managed to protest.

"Her bedroom, then. And be quick about it!"

Hiram swept me up as though I were weightless and in a few giant strides had reached my room. He laid me gently on the bed and stepped back; then Dulcie's worried face hung over me. I clutched at her.

"What is it, Miss Selina? Are you hurt, or did something scare you?"

I nodded. "Something...I think somebody was downstairs."

Instantly, Hiram was gone, and we could hear him running down the hall. Though my sobbing had lessened, I couldn't still the shuddering tremors that racked me.

"Sh, sh." Dulcie made soft, soothing sounds as she patted me. "Everything'll be all right. Hiram'll see to that."

I wish I had her confidence, I thought. I drew a deep, quivering breath.

"Dulcie, do you believe in ghosts?" The whispered words were out before I knew it, and at the look on her face I wished I might recall them. She actually blanched, leaving her skin a dirty tan.

"Why for you ask that? You think you seen a ghost, Miss Selina?" The comforting patting motion slowed.

"No, of course not," I said hastily. "It was just— Did my grandmother wear perfume a great deal? Any particular one, I mean."

Her eyes widened. "The ghost you seen was wearin' perfume?"

I decided I hadn't better mention the voice calling my name. "I didn't *see* a ghost, Dulcie. There was just a scent. I thought it might be attar of roses."

Relief returned the coffee color to her face. "And you feared it was Miss Raven—come back to haunt us?" She shook the turbaned head. "She never would have any kind of roses around. I think maybe they reminded her of Miss Rose."

As her words sank in, I closed my eyes. Could it have been my *mother's* voice that had called me so beseechingly? I hadn't given much thought to my mother. All the empathy I had felt had been for Raven.

We heard footsteps, and Hiram came back into the room. In answer to our inquiring looks, he shook his head. "Nothin' down there, nor no sign anybody been there. The doors and windows were all locked tight. Hadn't nobody been outside, neither, so far as I could tell." He shifted uneasily as he looked at me. "Same as all the times when somebody seen the little light."

"Has anybody ever *heard* anything?" I inquired tentatively.

He evaded my eyes. "Nothin' much. Jest a moan or two once on a while and mebbe some chains rattlin'."

Chains rattling? That time-worn, classic accompaniment to ghosts and spirits in tales told for hundreds of years! My terrors vanished. That sibilant whisper had come from no shade of my late grandmother or my mother but from someone bent on frightening me so thoroughly that I would leave this house and not come back. Only I hadn't the slightest idea why.

"No matter what you found, there *was* somebody downstairs," I said decisively. "I don't know how he got in, but I know it was a real person and not a ghost!"

I saw them exchange glances. "Then you're all right now?" Dulcie asked. "You don't want Hiram to go for Doc Gentry or Mr. Marcus?"

"Of course not." Then I added, trying not to let my voice falter, "But I would appreciate it, Hiram, if you would stay nearby the rest of the night."

"Don't you worry none about that. Anybody try to get to you is gonna have to step over me to do it!"

I slept well and soundly my first night at Raven's Rise and dreamed no dreams of ghosts and specters, or of anything at all.

DULCIE INSISTED that I have breakfast in bed after my ordeal, and I found it not difficult to humor her. I was just finishing my toast and second cup of coffee when I heard a commotion downstairs. A moment later, Marcus burst into my bedroom, with Dulcie hot on his heels. He came directly to my bed.

"Mr. Marcus, I told you you got no business barging into a lady's bedroom like this!" Dulcie was sputtering indignantly. "Why, you'll have the whole town talking about Miss Selina!"

"Since the *Bulletin* came out, the whole town talks of nothing else, anyhow," he said. "Selina, Hiram told me about last night, or as much as he knows of it. Why in heaven's name didn't you send him for me?"

I felt a little thrill of pleasure at the concern in his voice. "I didn't want to trouble you," I said, and added honestly, "Besides, I was too frightened to want to let him leave."

"Didn't want to trouble me! Dear girl, haven't I made it clear how I feel about you? What happened, anyway? Hiram says you heard someone downstairs, but he seems to think there's more to it than that."

I glanced at Dulcie, who was still hovering in the background.

"Dulcie, will you get Mr. Hannaford some coffee? And make it a fresh pot, please." I waited until she had left, not without a backward glance of disapproval. "There was someone downstairs, Marcus. I heard— Someone was whispering my name." As I said it, I could hear again that long, drawn-out sound, and my scalp prickled with remembered fear.

Marcus had sat on the step beside my bed, and at my words he reached over and gripped my arms tightly. "What do you mean? Who? And why, Selina?"

"I think somebody was trying to frighten me. Somebody who wants me out of this house." Haltingly, I went on to tell him what had happened and how I had been at first persuaded that it was Raven's spirit who had called to me. "But it wasn't, Marcus. I realized it when I heard that others had been frightened by groans and by the sound of chains rattling. It's ridiculous to think that grandmother's ghost would rattle chains. No, it's someone who wants to keep people away from this house. But why? Why would anyone want to do that?"

He didn't answer, but instead rose abruptly and exclaimed, "That settles it! You mustn't spend another night here. There's no telling what might happen next!"

I sat straight up in bed. "And let them win? Oh, no! I told you, Marcus, this is my house, and nobody is going to drive me from it!" I felt my cheeks blaze with excitement and anger. "Raven showed them all, and so will I!"

The angry light in Marcus's eyes faded, and an odd, speculative look replaced it. "What do you mean by that?"

"I—I'm not quite sure." It was true; the words had sprung unbidden to my lips. "It's just a sort of feeling I get—that it was her against the town."

"And if it was?" Marcus's tone was flat, almost stern. "Do you mean that you plan to continue the vendetta—without even knowing what it was all about?"

The disapproval in his voice made me stubborn. "If they push me to it. And I'll find out what it was, I know I will. The answer must be somewhere in this house."

"You are playing with fire, Selina," he warned me. Then he came again to sit beside my bed. "We love each other. Let's go on from there." He spoke coaxingly, and his warm hands captured mine. "These old grudges and old hates have nothing to do with us."

I found myself tempted by the persuasion in those soft hazel eyes. Then, slowly, I withdrew my hands from his.

"If you loved me," I said, and heard the inexorable note in my own voice, "you would want me to have what is rightfully mine."

He looked at me for a long moment. "And if you loved me," he said, his mouth set in a way I hadn't seen before, "you wouldn't jeopardize your safety and all that we could mean to each other by stirring up matters that would best be left undisturbed."

It was my turn to stare. At last, I said slowly, "You know, don't you? You know what lay between Raven Winfield and this town."

"I only know that whatever it was, it died with her. And it would be best left that way."

"Oh? Then why is someone still trying to drive me out of this house?"

"I don't know." I heard a trace of defeat. "But I think that by staying here you are putting yourself in terrible danger."

WHEN HE LEFT, the impasse was still between us. He was disturbed because of what he termed my obstinacy; I was frustrated and angry because I felt he was withholding from me information that I had a right to be privy to. The ethereal mood with which we had parted the previous night was almost blotted from my memory.

Almost. He had not been gone ten minutes before I wondered whether anything was important enough to separate us.

After Dulcie had removed my breakfast tray and tactfully withdrawn, I wandered disconsolately about my room for a while, then, with a sudden burst of energy, dressed and went downstairs. It was ridiculous to mope. I was an heiress, yet I hadn't explored half of my prized inheritance, nor had I spent a dollar of my riches. I decided to stroll to the bank, withdraw some cash and settle my account with Mr. Harper at the hotel. On my way back, I thought, it might be pleasant to stop in at the general store and select a gift for Ellie's mother in appreciation of her recent hospitality.

I spoke of my plans to Dulcie, who was dusting the library furniture.

"Before you get those plans too cut-and-dried," she said sagely, "you better take a look out of Miss Raven's window."

I glanced sharply at her, but she went on methodically dusting, so I hurried up to Raven's bedroom. There, clearly visible through the sheer curtains, was the main street, and it appeared to my shocked eyes that the entire town was gathering along it. Some, particularly the ladies, had taken pains to appear as though they were on legitimate business, with string-tied packages or shopping baskets on their arms; others had gathered in knots and were simply waiting. Even a few trees were festooned with barefoot youngsters who vied for the best vantage point from which to view any possible proceedings.

After my initial shock, the first emotion to strike me was anger. How dared they gather to gawk and whisper about me as though I were some circus-wagon freak? The second, following close upon its heels, was a delicious bubble of laughter. I hadn't seen more than ten people abroad at any given time since I had come to Bittercreek. How barren their lives must be, how lacking in the slightest flavoring of excitement, if the elevation of a quite ordinary young woman to the position of mistress of Raven's Rise could be cause for such commotion. I decided that it was only fair to humor them.

"You better be careful," Dulcie warned when I had told her of my intentions. "The people in this town don't have a sense of humor where Miss Raven is concerned. Ever since she built this place, they've been just plain jealous as if she didn't earn every stick and stone of it herself—"

"If they want to see me," I said obstinately, "they shall see me. I'll wager their opinions didn't keep my grandmother a prisoner in her own house."

She had to admit that they hadn't.

I returned to my room and performed as elaborate a toilette as was possible, considering the state of my wardrobe, then got my pocketbook and went downstairs.

Dulcie was in the entry hall, her feather dust momentarily at rest. As she looked me over from my head with its jaunty green bow to my white kid shoes, the tips of which just peeked from beneath my green-sprigged dress, the yellow cat's eyes narrowed.

"You look mighty fine," she said, "but if you want to come home again lookin' the same way, I'd advise you to take Hiram with you."

I refused to let her alarm me. "I hardly think I need a bodyguard in broad daylight," I said lightly. "I am simply going about the town upon matters of business, as any citizen might. I'll no doubt be back in an hour or so." Without waiting to hear another doleful remark, I quickly opened the front door and stepped out to the porch.

At my appearance a soft sound, as though a light breeze were soughing in the treetops, arose from the onlookers. I stood stock-still and let them look, not because I chose to but because my legs were suddenly weak beneath me.

After the communal sigh, a silence fell. I took a deep breath, commanded my quivering limbs to obey me and sailed off the porch and down the walk to the iron gate. As I reached it, Hiram appeared from nowhere to unlatch it, then stepped back to let me pass, his face a somber cloud.

"Thank you, Hiram," I said clearly. I nodded briskly to a nearby woman whose glance I caught, then started down the sidewalk as though it were the most natural thing in the world for half the citizens of Bittercreek to be gathered along it.

It was the longest walk I had ever taken, that short stroll from the gates of Raven's Rise to the veranda of the hotel. I didn't know what to expect—catcalls, rude noises, mud balls thrown or tobacco juice spit—none of these would have surprised me.

What did surprise me was the utter silence. Not one person spoke—either in greeting or with hostility—and those whose glance I inadvertently met looked quickly away, only, I guessed, to stare again when I had passed. It wasn't until I had nearly reached my destination that the silence was broken, and that by a boy of seven or so who was walking toward me with his mother. His voice rose shrilly as he asked, "Ma, is that lady Miss Winfield's bas—"

His mother's hand caught him smartly across the mouth, and startled and dismayed, I looked at her in protest. Her plain face was expressionless, but in her eyes I read hostility. As we met, she moved her skirts aside to let me pass, as though my very touch might contaminate her.

Utter defeat swept over me. What had I done, what had Raven done, that these people should feel this way about us? I think in another moment I would have run weeping into the dubious shelter of the hotel if Dr. Gentry hadn't hailed me from the dining-room door.

"Well, Miss Ames!" He came toward me with his ambling gait. "Out for a morning constitutional?"

"Dr. Gentry!" My eyes grew moist at the sight of his kindly smile. "Why, not exactly. I plan to do a little shopping."

"I don't suppose it could wait a spell? It would be nice to have a pretty young woman to chat with over a cup of coffee."

We were both aware that our every word was being heard by the nearby onlookers.

"Thank you, doctor. But I would like to get to the bank before it closes for the noon hour. Might I ask you instead to come to tea this afternoon at Raven's Rise?"

He nodded. "Even better. Around four? Raven usually had tea around that time."

"That will be fine. And, Dr. Gentry," I added softly, "thank you."

He tipped his hat and stepped back into the dining room. With my spirits restored, I went briskly across the street to the bank. Mr. Soames was standing just inside the door, trying to look as though he hadn't been peering out the window at my approach. He greeted me effusively.

"My dear Miss Ames! How can I help you on this bright and cheery morning?" As he spoke, he took my elbow and guided me to the chair beside his desk.

"I only wish to withdraw a small amount of cash from my account," I told him. "I'm sure the young man at the wicket could help me with it."

"And deprive me of the privilege of serving one of our most valued stockholders?" He had taken his place opposite me, and now he leaned across the desk and playfully shook a pudgy finger. "It was sly of you not to tell me that first day that you were Miss Winfield's granddaughter."

I liked him even less in this jocular mood than I had before, and I wondered what he would say if I answered truthfully that I hadn't even known it. Instead, I said, "I am afraid I was not yet at liberty to do that."

"Of course, of course." He rubbed fat hands together. "Now, how much do you want, and which account would you like it drawn from?"

"I think fifty dollars would suffice, and I would like it taken from my own account." Though Marcus had told me there was money here ready for my use, I had been too overwhelmed to grasp the particulars. Besides, I wasn't yet accustomed to thinking of it as mine. "I wish to clear up my bill with Mr. Harper, and I have a few small purchases to make."

"My dear, is that all? There is no need to trouble yourself, you know. All you must do is direct that the bills for any purchases be sent here and they will be promptly paid. The bank is happy to take those little annoyances off your hands."

"No, thank you. I prefer to pay my own bills and keep my own accounts, just as my grandmother did."

At these words he seemed to deflate considerably.

"Oh, of course. I— It is just that Raven Winfield was an experienced businesswoman, whereas you—" His eyes did not quite meet mine.

"—are young and possibly quite naive." I finished the sentence for him. "You may be right, but I intend to emulate my grandmother as nearly as is possible."

He did meet my eyes then, and I thought he looked a little ill. What could I have said? Even though I didn't care for the man, I wanted to make amends for whatever it had been, so as I rose, I added graciously, "I would be pleased if you would care to come to tea."

If anything, he looked even sicker.

"I would be delighted." He swallowed. "May I ask when?"

I thought I might as well get it over. "This afternoon would be fine. About five? I understand that is the hour at which you usually visited grandmother."

"Five." He said it dully. "Yes. That would do as well as any."

I waited, and he stood gazing as though he didn't really see me. "The fifty dollars?" I prompted him.

"Oh! I'm terribly sorry." Quickly, he got the money and brought it to me. We touched hands, said the usual amenities, and I left.

I glanced back once as I was going to the general store two doors down. He had come out on the walk to watch me go, and he was pressing a square of snow-white handkerchief against his upper lip.

But his were not the only eyes that watched me. As far as I could tell, none of the loiterers on the walks had so much as changed position. Even though I had concluded by now that they intended no overt hostility, I was happy to reach the door of the general store.

There was no one inside when I entered except a balding, middle-aged man who was stacking shelves.

He craned around as I came in, then climbed down with some deliberation and turned to face me. I could see by the conjecture in his eyes that he was assuming my identity. He nodded without committing himself to friendliness.

"Can I help you, ma'am?"

Determined to coax a kindly response from somebody—other, of course, than Mr. Soames—I smiled pleasantly and took a deep, testing sniff. The air was redolent of spices. "Mmm! It smells so good in here!" I said. "I want to buy some of whatever is producing that delightful odor!"

His lips twitched in a grudging smile. "That's my wife's cinnamon bread. We live in the back, and she just baked this morning. I reckon I can let you have a loaf if you're serious."

"Very serious. It sounds just the thing to go with tea this afternoon." I hoped Dulcie would forgive me. "But I also want to look around. I am interested in a small gift for a lady."

"Let's see." I could tell that his attitude was warming toward me. "How about a shawl? Got some nice ones on the shelf up front."

"It is a little warm for that, I think." I was glancing over the displays as I spoke. "Do you have any scented soap?"

"I surely do. Right over there with the perfume." He reached the counter ahead of me and proudly displayed a quite pretty box of oval lavender soaps. "Imported all the way from England. Used to be Miss Winfield's favorite." He bit the last word off abruptly, as though too late aware of what he had said.

I held the box to my nose and sniffed delicately. "Very nice. I'd like this, please." I handed it to him, and then, because the flowerlike aroma had reminded me of last night, asked casually, "Do you by chance stock a perfume called attar of roses?"

"Attar of roses?" He thought a moment. "By golly, I do think we got a bottle of it on the shelf back there. Been here a long time, though. Nobody seems to be wanting it anymore." As he spoke, he went behind the central counter and reached toward an upper shelf, but his hand froze in midair before an empty space. "Well, I'll be. It's gone. Wife must've sold it. I'd ask her, but she's out—" He stopped, embarrassed. Out waiting to gawk at me, apparently. "I could order you some," he continued lamely.

"Oh, don't bother. I'm sure you have another fragrance that will do." I chose another almost at random, then wandered about selecting a few more items: an embroidered handkerchief, a filmy scarf, a plump pincushion, more of the lavender soap—partly because the man had been civil and partly because it seemed so wonderful to buy something frivolous without counting the cost.

The amount he charged seemed staggering, but I paid it without demur while feeling quite wickedly extravagant. He offered to have the items delivered, but I insisted on waiting while he wrapped each one and tied it with string. Part of the fun was arriving home with one's purchases; besides, I meant to deliver Mrs. Henderson's soap as I passed her house.

After stowing the packages in a string bag that he wanted to give me but for which I insisted on paying the requisite two cents, I went back outside. My mind was on that missing bottle of attar of roses, and I didn't notice at first that the knots of people were, albeit reluctantly, breaking up and apparently going about their own concerns. When it did occur to me, I glanced about for the reason but could see none, though Mr. Soames was still standing at the entrance to his bank.

CHAPTER TEN

THOUGH I THOUGHT that it seemed somewhat forced, Mr. Harper was no less surly than before as I settled my account. I found that I admired him for it. At least he hadn't succumbed to fawning, as Mr. Soames had, now that he knew I was Raven's heir, though I felt that my relief at our parting was shared by him.

Mrs. Henderson was guardedly pleased to see me. I didn't know whether her attitude was self-conscious because of the number of people who were still covertly watching or because she feared the town's reaction to our friendship. I soon discovered that it had a little to do with both.

"My land," she remarked as she showed me, this time, into her little parlor, "you'd think those people would have something better to do than to stand around gossiping, wouldn't you? Why, I'll bet half of 'em don't have their houses swept yet." She bustled about, settling me comfortably, then took the chair opposite. "Envy is a terrible thing, Miss Ames. It can make people downright mean."

"I know," I said. "Perhaps I shouldn't have come. I only wanted to thank you for your hospitality the other day. And to bring you this." I retrieved the wrapped parcel of soap from my shopping bag and handed it to her.

She took it with an air of surprise and began to untie the string. After unwrapping the package she gasped with pleasure. "Why, these are lovely! And so nice-smelling, too." As she looked at me, her eyes were moist. "There wasn't any need for it, though. I didn't do anything but be neighborly."

"That's something not too common in Bittercreek, I find." I hesitated, then asked impulsively, "Mrs. Henderson, do you have any idea why someone would want to break into Raven's Rise?" As she glanced quickly at me, I added, "I have heard that they have done so in the past."

She looked down at the brown paper she was thriftily smoothing and folding. "You can hear most anything when money's involved. But it's pretty certain that something funny has been going on at the mansion ever since Miss Winfield died. Some say it's thieves, though nothing seems to have come up missing, but other folks swear that it's ghosts guarding the place." She looked up at me. "Either way, I think it's got something to do with the treasure."

A small chill ran over me. "Treasure?" I faltered.

She gave a little sigh, then went on as though prepared to reveal an unpleasant truth. "You may as well know. Some silly fools in this town have got it in their heads that Miss Winfield had a lot more money than has turned up in her investments and in the bank. They think she hid it somewhere in that monster house of hers." She shook her head disparagingly. "Far as I'm concerned, she had better sense, but you know how folks are. Everybody wants something for nothing, if he can get it."

I sat quite still, absorbing this, for it explained a lot of things. Someone most seriously did believe in the tale of treasure, and to that person I was definitely in the way. I had no doubt been correct last night when I had decided that somebody was trying to frighten me away. It also revealed to me the puzzle of the townspeople's initial hostility. If I had not appeared to claim the property, the town would have inherited it, and the city fathers would have been free to search at leisure for whatever might be hidden there.

And true or not, it posed a serious problem, for I wouldn't be left in peace until I had disproved it.

Or proved it by finding a treasure. There was always that.

Mrs. Henderson was watching me, her face puckered with sympathy. I could see that she grasped my difficulty. How could one *disprove* the existence of a treasure?

The older woman stirred, and I realized that I had been sitting silently for several moments. "Thank you for telling me this," I said. "It clears up a good deal of confusion in my mind. And please, will you and Ellie come to see me? You are almost my only friends in Bittercreek."

She looked a little overwhelmed but said staunchly, "We certainly will. In the meantime, you just stop by anytime. And you don't need to bring a present, either."

We parted with good feelings on both sides, and I was able to ignore the remaining onlookers as I covered the short distance between her cottage and Raven's Rise.

DULCIE SEEMED almost annoyed that her dire predictions hadn't come true, but was mollified by my gift of the embroidered handkerchief.

"Well, I'd of sworn you'd come home with tobacco juice spit all over you, if nothing more," she said. "Those people out there looked set for meanness." She admired the handkerchief extravagantly, then tucked it in her belt. "Thank you, Miss Selina, that was mighty thoughtful."

"I think perhaps Mr. Soames discouraged them," I said. "They began to disperse after he came out to the street. By the way, he is coming to tea at five. Oh! And Dr. Gentry at four." I had just remembered inviting the doctor. "But I bought a loaf of cinnamon bread which you can use. The storekeeper's wife had just been baking."

She gave a disdainful sniff as I handed it to her. "I'll take care of something to serve. Don't you worry about that." She slanted a look at me. "This tea party going to take place in the library or the parlor?"

This time I caught my cue. "Where would you suggest?" I asked innocently.

"Dr. Gentry, the library. Banker Soames, the parlor." Her answer was instant and decisive.

"I see," I said slowly. But I didn't, quite. Apparently, the good friends were accorded the comfortable library; others—those Raven had disliked—the parlor. But if she hadn't liked Soames and his erstwhile mining partners, why did she entertain them at all? And since these things were usually mutual, why had they been such faithful callers?

I remembered that I had not yet looked for the appointment books of earlier years. Laying my other purchases on the hall table, I started toward the library.

"Aren't you going to have lunch, Miss Selina?" Dulcie called after me.

"Just bring a sandwich in here, will you, Dulcie? I remembered something I meant to do."

When she came in with a small tray of food, I was still searching along the rows of books. "Something I can help you with?" she asked.

"Possibly. I found an appointment book in grandmother's bedroom desk. Do you know if she kept the others—from earlier years?"

"Sure she did." She rubbed her forehead with bony fingers. "Seems like I saw them last time I dusted in here." Her eyes roamed over the shelves. Suddenly, she exclaimed, "I remember! They're in that bottom cupboard over there. Want me to get them for you?"

My glance followed her pointing finger. "I'll get them. I know you have things to do."

After she had gone, I went to kneel before the cupboard doors. I noticed that my breath had quickened as I reached to open the small brass latch and wondered at my excitement. Did I really think that I was about to find some answer, some clue at least, to the mystery that seemed to envelop Raven's Rise?

At my touch the cupboard doors swung open to reveal leather-bound books that matched the one I had found in grandmother's desk. My excitement grew as

I saw there were more of them than I had dared to hope. I counted swiftly. Sixteen! That meant that if each comprised a year, as did the one upstairs, then the first was begun in 1854, the year the house had been built. And I would have, if nothing more, a clear account of her activities during those years.

As I lifted them out by twos and threes, a spurt of dust set me to sneezing. I supposed they had not been touched since they had been set there at the end of each year. Piling them carefully one atop the other, I carried them over to the comfortable chair beside my luncheon tray.

A long time later, the tray still stood untouched, the tea cold, the dainty sandwiches dried and curling at the edges. I had carefully searched all the books—from 1854 through 1869. Raven had had many visitors in that time, far more than I would have expected. A few were names known to me; most, who appeared sporadically through the years, were not. The most frequent names listed were those of Dr. Gentry and Marcus's father in earlier years, and Marcus's own the last several. But the only two names to appear on set dates and at regular intervals were those of Mr. Soames and Mayor Ogilvey and, apparently when he was in residence in Bittercreek, Senator Hogarth Bentley. Their visits had taken place immediately after Raven had built the house and begun keeping appointment books, and just three years after she had made her bitter accusations of the partners concerning the death of her lover, Will Prentiss.

It simply did not make sense.

I was still sitting with the last book on my lap when Dulcie came in to announce Dr. Gentry's arrival. The doctor, who was right behind her, began an immediate apology.

"I know I'm a little early, Miss Ames, but I'm likely to have to go out again. Mrs. O'Brian's third is on the way." He gave a little sigh of weariness as he settled into a comfortable chair near mine. "Feels good to be sitting here again. I miss my visits with Raven."

"Judging from these appointment books," I told him, "you were her closest friend."

The bushy eyebrows knit. "Appointment books? Didn't know she kept any. If she's got it down there every time I came visiting, I guess it would look like it." He nodded, thinking about it. "And I guess it'd be true, too, after Jake died. She and Marcus's pa were partners, you know, way back when."

I said carefully, "She seemed to have several loyal friends. Mayor Ogilvey and Mr. Soames were exceedingly regular in their visits."

"Yes, I guess they were. Well, will you look at that cake! Dulcie, you sure know the way to a man's heart!"

He seemed quite genuinely interested in Dulcie and the tea tray, but I wondered if he had deliberately changed the subject. I waited until we each had our tea and cake, then brought it up again.

"It was surprising, under the circumstances."

"What was? Oh, you mean Ogilvey and Soames? I don't know why. They had all known each other almost from Bittercreek's beginning."

"Yes, but she had accused them of murder, Dr. Gentry. It seems to me that would be a hard thing to overlook."

It appeared for a moment that Dulcie's chocolate cake had lost its flavor. "Where'd you get that little nugget of information? Carrie Henderson?"

"I found it in the *Bittercreek Bulletin*—when I was searching for some clue as to who I was."

The bushy eyebrows knit again. "Look, Miss Ames—"

"Selina," I interposed.

"Selina, they just let bygones be bygones, I guess. And it might not be a bad idea for you, either. No good is going to come of raking over the past, stirring up things that might best be forgotten."

"Marcus has been talking to you," I said bitterly.

"No, he hasn't," he said, suddenly irate. "Well, he has, but it had nothing to do with this. Nobody admired Raven Winfield more than I did, but she's gone now, and it's over. And you've got what you wanted— you know who you are and who your parents were. And that's all you need to know. Be happy with it and go on with your life."

I set down my untouched tea and cake. "You are wrong on two counts," I said. "It's not over, and if Marcus told you about last night, you know it's not. As for my grandmother, I want to know all there is to know about her—what she thought and what she felt and what kept her going after she had lost everything that had made life worthwhile. And most of all, I want to know what it is that you and Marcus don't want me to find out."

With deliberation, Dr. Gentry ate the last bite of his cake and finished his tea, then carefully wiped his mustache with his napkin.

"Did you ever stop to think that maybe Raven wouldn't want you to know? That maybe she wouldn't appreciate you prying into her affairs, into her feelings, into her innermost thoughts? She was a very private person, Selina. Even I didn't always know what she was thinking or how she felt about things. And she wanted it that way. For all you know, maybe she still does." He got up then, and I rose with him. "I'd better be getting down to Mrs. O'Brian's before she finds out she can manage without me."

I didn't want our visit to end like this.

"Please," I said, "don't you see that searching into Raven's past is the only way I have of learning my own? I had hoped I could count on you to supply some of the missing pieces."

He shook his head. "My business is with the living, and so should yours be. Sell this place and leave Bittercreek," he advised not unkindly. "That's my prescription for a happy life."

With that he was gone, and I was left to my own confused thoughts. How *would* Raven have felt about it? Would she, as the doctor had said, resent my prying into her past affairs? Or was there some situation that her unexpected death had left unresolved?

As Dulcie came in to get the tea tray, she eyed my gown, which I had not changed since going out that morning. "If Mr. Soames won't be here until five, you'll have time to change, won't you?" It was more a hint than a question.

"I'm sure I will," I answered. Then, impulsively, I asked, "Dulcie, did grandmother like Mr. Soames and Mr. Ogilvey?"

She became very busy collecting the tea things. "I'm sure I wouldn't know, Miss Selina. Miss Raven never said." Before I could phrase another question, she swept up the tray and left the library.

I didn't immediately go upstairs, but went instead to gaze up at Raven's portrait. "Well, grandmother, what about it?" I asked aloud. "Are you angry with me for trying to meddle into your affairs? Or am I right in feeling that there is something here that needs attending to, something that you didn't get a chance to put to rights before you had to go?"

There was no change of expression in the dark eyes that looked serenely into mine, but I seemed to feel a benign warmth envelop me. Its solace was so great that I closed my eyes and for a moment imagined that I caught the delicate scent of lavender.

Much cheered and with my determination strengthened, I went upstairs to change for tea with Mr. Soames.

CHAPTER ELEVEN

WHEN MR. SOAMES RANG MY DOORBELL promptly at five, I was surprised to find that he was not alone. He introduced as Mayor Harold Ogilvey the spare, rather cadaverous-appearing man who accompanied him.

"I hope you don't mind me tagging along," the mayor said, "but I have been wanting to meet you."

"Not at all," I answered graciously, and meant it. I was curious to meet this other partner who had been so faithful a visitor to my grandmother, and seeing the two men together might be even more interesting. I dismissed Dulcie, who had answered the door, and led the way into the parlor. I hadn't been in this room since the day I had first seen the emerald ring in Raven's portrait, and I was again overwhelmed by its elegant clutter.

It seemed to affect the two partners the same way, and they perched uneasily in the slippery satin chairs.

"Well, well, Miss Ames!" Mr. Soames began with his ponderous joviality. "How do you think you are going to like being mistress of Raven's Rise?" In spite of the smile that accompanied this, I thought that he seemed nervous.

"I don't know," I answered with deliberate candor. "I have scarcely had a chance to explore it yet. It *is* nice knowing I will never be in want again." I was not revealing any secrets of my past; after Jared's newspaper article, every soul in Bittercreek knew of my erstwhile penurious state. However, I did catch the quick glance that flashed between them.

"The *Bulletin* had quite a story on you," Mayor Ogilvey said, echoing my thoughts. "Have you any idea of the identity of this benefactor who urged you to come here?" He spoke casually, as though he were making idle conversation, but I immediately bridled.

"I try not to speculate about it," I said stiffly. "I owe so much to this person, and he or she obviously doesn't want to be identified. I feel the least I can do is honor that wish."

"Of course, of course. And very commendable." I noticed a light sheen of perspiration on Mr. Soames's forehead as he cast a disparaging look at the mayor. "It is just that we would like to give this person a vote of thanks for causing justice to be done and for adding such a beautiful young lady to our town's population."

It was such obvious hokum that even Mayor Ogilvey stirred uneasily. *You really would like to run whoever it is out of town on a rail,* I thought with sudden insight. *And me, too, if you dared.* But I said gravely, "It is kind of you to take that attitude. I am aware that Bittercreek lost a great deal by my coming to claim my grandmother's estate."

Mayor Ogilvey spoke before the banker could form another insincere protest.

"I'll admit it was a blow of sorts. You surely agree that Raven's Rise is ideally situated for a town hall."

He hesitated, then went on. "In fact, one of my reasons for coming today was to ask if you would consider selling it to us."

I had not expected that, and it sent my thoughts whirling. How could a place the size of Bittercreek justify such an expenditure? And why did they feel the need of so large and splendid a structure when they had obviously gotten along all these years without it? I could only conclude that they believed the rumors of a treasure and planned to search for it.

Fortunately, Dulcie came in with the tea tray just then, giving me time to phrase a judicious answer.

"I do appreciate your interest in Raven's Rise," I said after tea and cookies had been handed around, "but at the present time I have no intention of selling. I plan to live here indefinitely, just as my grandmother did, and to keep everything exactly as she had it."

Again I noted the look that passed between them.

"Everything?" Mr. Soames faltered.

"Perhaps not everything," I amended slowly. There were undercurrents here that I couldn't fathom. "But certainly the important things. I have set myself to learn all that I can about her and her life in Bittercreek. I have already realized that this town and the people in it were very important to her. She could have lived anywhere, you know, after she closed her business, yet she chose to stay here for the remainder of her life. Just as you gentlemen have."

I had no idea why my words seemed to disturb them, but the mayor began to fidget as though his chair seat had grown uncomfortably warm, and Mr.

Soames found it necessary to blot the perspiration on his upper lip. Neither man would quite meet my eyes. At last Mayor Ogilvey said, "You don't think that you will find things...uninteresting after a while?"

Ah, I thought, another person who wishes to discourage my staying here. Aloud I said, "That remains to be seen. I can always visit San Francisco from time to time as grandmother did."

Again an uncomfortable silence ensued. At last Mr. Soames said, "Naturally, you should do as you wish." He set his teacup down and rose. "I'm afraid that we must be going. Our wives will be expecting us for dinner. Is there—" He was again perspiring, and he cast another rather desperate glance at the mayor. "Is there anything we can do for you right at the moment?"

I smiled to conceal my confusion. "Why, not at the moment. But if there is, I shall certainly let you know."

The two men stiffened at my words, and Mr. Soames licked lips gone suddenly dry.

"You do that, Miss Ames," he mumbled, again without meeting my eyes. "Be glad to oblige."

Mayor Ogilvey muttered a similar response, and with an unmistakable air of escaping, they quickly departed.

I returned to my chair, which was large and ornate and seemingly the only comfortable one in the room. In fact, I realized, it was actually built with a higher seat than was normal, and the fan-shaped back gave one a sense of being seated on a throne. I couldn't help smiling to myself. I believe you *were* a bit wicked, grandmother, I decided. No wonder those men didn't like you.

Immediately, I stopped to consider the thought. Why had I come to that conclusion? They hadn't spoken one word of disparagement, yet I had felt their antipathy toward her. That they also didn't care for me, I had supposed to be because of my untimely appearance in Bittercreek, but what if there was more to it than that? What if Raven had been somehow compelling them to visit her, had been—

I broke off, laughing at myself. If Marcus knew of my imaginings, he would remove me from this house by bodily force, if necessary. But ridiculous or not, I could not rid myself of the feeling that throughout their brief visit Soames and Ogilvey had been waiting—dreading—something that they feared might come from me.

I could not imagine what it could have been.

AFTER DINNER, which I ate in solitary grandeur while Dulcie served, I returned to the library. Had it really been only last night that Marcus and I had been so happy here? He had been angry this morning, but I knew it had only been because he worried about me, and all day I had half expected him to reappear and greet me with that slow, teasing smile that had at first infuriated, and now delighted, me. But I knew so little about him. Perhaps, I thought, and felt my heart grow heavy, he was the type of man who could not forgive a woman for having opinions of her own. If so, our romance was doomed from the beginning, for my early life had taught me that the only way to survive with dignity was by developing an independent nature.

I wandered restlessly about the library, then returned to Raven's appointment books. But when leafing through them garnered no more information, I took them back to the cupboard beneath the shelves.

As I tried to fit the last book against the wooden side panel, it caught at the top. Reaching in, I ran my hand along the upper edge of the panel and found a small protruding nail that seemed to have come loose. I tried to push it back in, and failing that, gave it a little tug. The nail came out easily, but as it did so, the entire end panel of the cupboard slid down, revealing a shallow aperture in the wall.

I stared in astonishment; then a slow excitement rose in me. The niche quite obviously had been built as a place of concealment, and though in this shadowy corner of the room I could see nothing hidden there, I gingerly reached inside. My groping fingers encountered a cold, hard cylinder of some sort. Eagerly, I seized it and drew it into the light. No larger than a cigar and of about the same color, it appeared to be a paper, or papers, that had been wrapped in oilskin.

I remained on my knees before the cupboard for a long moment. Dread began to override the excitement I had felt at first. Within this packet might be the answer to the mystery of Raven's Rise, and at this crucial moment I wasn't at all sure I was ready to learn it. At last I shut the cupboard doors and returned to my chair, where I removed the outer oilskin covering, and after pulling the lamp closer, unrolled the paper cylinder.

I saw that it was not one but three documents, the largest a crude map drawn on wrapping paper with a blunt pencil. The scrawled names of river and trails meant nothing to me, but I noticed with a sense of shock that beside a large X were the words "Claim Here." The second paper was a report from an assayer's office, and while I didn't understand the notations, it was as though the clear, bold signature at the bottom leaped at me from the past.

Henry Ames.

The third piece of paper was a letter written on that same brown wrapping paper:

Dear Raven,

Can't wait for you any longer, dearest. I have got to get to the claims office. Here's proof of my strike, just like I told you. Soames and the others will never believe I found it after we broke up, but they can do nothing when I have filed. I think they suspect, so if anything happens to me, take these papers to the sheriff. Henry will back you up. He knows the truth.

Hope you find this okay. I love you.

It was signed simply "Will."

I let the papers drop into my lap.

Will. Will Prentiss, Raven's lover, whom she had accused the erstwhile partners of murdering. And Henry Ames, my father, who, according to this letter, had known the truth.

I was stunned by the import of these papers, but dimly I realized that no one, not even Dulcie, ought to know of their existence. With numb, awkward fingers I rewrapped them in the oilskin cover and replaced them in their hidden niche, then sank into my chair and sat staring into the empty fireplace. I had the pieces of the puzzle now; I simply needed to put them together.

If the location of the Four Horsemen Mine was the same as that on the hidden map, then Raven had been right, I decided. Will had discovered it first and quite possibly had been killed by the partners because of it. But why, then, at the time of her accusation of them, hadn't she taken these papers along to verify it?

Hope you find this okay.

But she hadn't found them yet, apparently. He probably had hidden them all too well. When she had demanded a hearing, she must have had as her only proof a secret witness, who subsequently failed to appear. And that, I realized with bitter contempt, would have been Henry Ames, who had slunk out of town under cover of darkness rather than face the consequences of his own lascivious behavior.

Raven had continued for three more years to run the Red Garter Saloon before selling her share to Marcus's father; it was after that that she had built Raven's Rise. And it was then that the partners had become her faithful friends. Why? What could have happened to turn things around so completely?

She had finally found Will's papers.

I was flooded with sudden understanding. In the intervening years, the partners, wealthy from the proceeds of the stolen mine, had no doubt become important men in the community, even in the state. And then Raven had discovered the means to brand them thieves and murderers and to ruin their lives as they had ruined hers.

Yet she had not done it. Why?

There was only one answer, and my bones turned to water as the enormity of it overwhelmed me. She had found a better way to punish them. My grandmother must have been blackmailing Soames and his partners for seventeen long years.

What I meant by the word "blackmail" I could not decide. I only felt that she had made them pay, somehow, for Will's death and for all the pain and empty years that death had caused her. She must have insisted that they appear before her twice each month, had even, for that matter, made them command their unwilling wives to do her bidding, to come to Raven's Rise and sit at dinner, to make polite conversation with a woman they despised, on pain of disclosure and public scandal. And today it had been fear that I had sensed in my meeting with Ogilvey and Soames, fear that I had somehow learned their secret and planned to continue controlling them as Raven had.

I thought again about those twice-monthly visits. They must have had a purpose to Raven beyond that of watching the men writhe in her trap. Each of them had come alone, I remembered, never the two of them together, as they had today. Had she forced them to spy on each other and then report? Or had she gone so far as to actually demand money?

I thought about that, too. This house itself, its lavish ornamentation, the yearly trips to San Francisco, even the generosity she apparently had displayed on many occasions—could she have actually done that well even with her gambling establishment and her clever business investments together? Or had she found a sure and inexhaustible way to supplement her income?

Dulcie knocked gently and then came in.

"Can I get you something before Hiram and I go to bed, Miss Selina? Some coffee, maybe?"

I tried to rouse myself. "No, thank you, Dulcie." I felt a chill run over me. "A small fire would be nice, though, if it isn't too much trouble."

"No trouble at all, but it sure don't seem cold in here." She took a few sticks of wood from the bin and knelt at the hearth. In a moment the fire had kindled and lit. "You aren't coming down with something, are you?"

I tried to smile as, gratefully, I welcomed the warmth of the blaze against my hands.

"I don't think so. I've probably been sitting still too long."

She regarded me. "I think I'll close the drapes," she said. "Maybe there's a draft coming in around the windows."

I wasn't even aware of when she left the room. I was absorbed in the likeness of Raven that watched me from over the mantel. She had been so beautiful, so graceful, so utterly serene. How much pain she must have suffered to have turned into the bitter, ruthless woman she had become!

"Was it worth it, grandmother?" I whispered at last. "Even though they killed him, did punishing them make the pain any less?"

Our eyes met, and it was as though disappointment clouded her clear gaze. *I thought you, at least, would understand,* she seemed to say.

I'm trying, grandmother. I really am, I answered silently. *If it wasn't the money or simply that you wanted them to suffer, then what was it all for? What did you really expect to gain from it?*

I have no idea how long I sat looking into my grandmother's lovely face as the fire whispered secrets that I could not fathom; how long before I realized that it was not the gaze from her painted eyes that was raising gooseflesh along my arms. I stirred uneasily, and a chill of fear went down my spine.

Someone in this room was watching me.

CHAPTER TWELVE

I COULDN'T CREDIT MY SENSES at first. It wasn't possible. The room had no closet, no hiding space. The draperies were drawn tightly across each window. Yet it persisted—that eerie, terrifying certainty that unseen eyes were watching me.

I sat quite still, my eyes riveted on Raven's portrait. I was gripped so strongly by fear that at first I dared not move. Then I thought of last night, of that sibilant whisper enticing me, coaxing me to believe that her ghost was waiting for me here.

The memory released me from my paralyzed state, and I knew what I must do. I let my eyes droop and close a time or two, as though I were being overcome by sleep; then I stretched and yawned elaborately. Taking my time, I rose and yawned again as I leisurely crossed to the hall door. But once outside that door, I slammed it shut and stood with my back against it while I shouted loudly for Dulcie and Hiram.

"Quickly, quickly!" I screamed as they raced down the long hall toward me. "He's in there, Hiram, in the library!"

Without hesitation, Hiram tore open the library door and disappeared inside.

"Lordy, Miss Selina, was it the ghost again?" Dulcie, looking like a ghost herself in her long white nightgown, hovered distractedly over me.

"S-somebody was staring at me!" I almost wailed. "I could feel it, Dulcie. I really could. Hiram—?"

He had come to the doorway, and as I looked inquiringly at him, he regretfully shook his head. "There ain't nobody in there a'tall, Miss Selina. The windows was all locked on the inside, like always, and I looked behind the curtains. There just ain't no place else to hide."

"But there has to be!" I insisted. "I could feel his eyes—watching me!" I shuddered at the memory.

I saw the look they exchanged.

"You don't believe me, do you?" My teeth had begun to chatter. "You think that I'm—that I'm—"

"Oh, no, Miss Selina. We—" The jangling of the doorbell interrupted Dulcie. "Now who could that be?" she muttered in exasperation. With one more anxious look at me, she went to open the door. "Why, Mr. Newcomb!" I heard her say. "How come you're calling at this hour?"

"I know it's late, but I saw the lights...." Jared's warm voice answered her. "I wondered if Miss Ames..." The door swung wider, and he saw me standing there. "Oh, Selina, may I—" His voice changed, sharpened. "What's wrong?" He pushed the door open and strode toward me. "My dear girl, whatever is the matter?"

I was quivering from head to foot. "It—it's nothing," I managed to say. "I—I fell asleep before the fire. A nightmare—" I couldn't bear to tell him the truth and see the concern in his eyes change to uneasy conjecture. "I'm just overtired, I think. But if you wouldn't mind—some other time—"

"Of course. If you're sure there's nothing I can do."

Dulcie was already easing him toward the door.

"If there is, we'll surely let you know, Mr. Newcomb. 'Night, now.'' He went reluctantly, and she shut the door firmly behind him and hurried back to me. "Child, you're freezing to death! We've got to get you to bed!"

"But what about—"

"Hiram will lock the library door from this side. If there is anybody in there, he can't get out again except by the window. We can worry about it in the morning."

She jerked her head at Hiram. As she helped me up the stairs, I glanced over my shoulder. He was just slipping through the outer door.

With Dulcie murmuring soothing words and helping me as though I were a child, I readied for bed and slid gratefully beneath the covers. It was the impossibility of the thing that frightened me so. If the draperies had not been drawn, I would have shrugged it off as a curious neighbor or Peeping Tom, but as it was, I was almost forced to doubt my own senses, to fear that my preoccupation with Raven's problems had caused me to imagine it.

As my shuddering chills lessened under Dulcie's deft ministrations, I considered that last. I wasn't at all sure that she wasn't here, I decided. Though never before a believer in ghostly spirits, since coming to Raven's Rise, I had often, almost without acknowledging it, felt a benign presence. But my grandmother, spirit or no, would not frighten me as I had been frightened by that presence in the library. There had been nothing benign about it, and it had been very, very real.

Though I would have forbidden him to do it had I known, I wasn't sorry to find that Hiram had fetched Dr. Gentry. The first sight of the doctor's kindly, tired face brought tears rushing to my eyes.

"Now, here, here," he soothed after climbing the steps to my bed and perching on its edge. "Are you really that sorry to see me?" But the way I clutched his hands and bit back sobs must have convinced him that this was no time for joking, for he immediately sent the two servants from the room. "Now," he said, "I'm going to give you a swallow of something to calm you down, and then you can tell me what this is all about." His black bag was beside him, and he rummaged in it, eventually producing a vial of colorless liquid. "Just drink this right down. I guarantee it'll cure what ails you."

I obeyed him without argument. Whatever it was, it seemed to work like magic, for I grew calmer almost immediately. After a moment, I told him what had happened. "You believe me, don't you, Dr. Gentry?" I asked anxiously. "I don't think Dulcie does, but you don't think I'm imagining things, do you?"

His long silence made me uneasy. "I'll tell you the truth, Selina," he said at last. "When I first met you, I would have said that you'd be the last person to imagine a thing like this. But a lot has happened since then, and you've been under considerable strain. What with all the changes in your life, even if they're for the better, and you coming to live in this spooky old house—well, I think most anybody might crack a little under it." He raised a hand to ward off my protestations. "Don't get mad, now. I'm just saying that I think there is a chance that you imagined it."

"But I didn't," I insisted stubbornly. "Someone was watching me—someone real, someone alive. It seems impossible, but it's true."

He nodded. "All right. Let's say that you have me convinced. What are you going to do about it?"

"I...what can I do?"

"You can move out of here." He spoke almost sternly. "You can rent a room at the hotel or stay with Ellie's mother—or go back to San Francisco, which probably would be the wisest. But whether you're right about tonight or whether you imagined it, this isn't a healthy atmosphere for you."

I felt my lips tighten. "This is my home," I said. "Why should I have to leave it?"

"Because if you don't—" he leaned toward me and tapped a stubby forefinger on the counterpane "—word'll get out that you're going daft. And it *will* get out, believe me. That's one of the curses of a small town. When it does, it will be the best excuse in the world for someone to step forward, sue to have you committed and grab himself the juicy spot of manager of your estate. Much more of these nighttime hysterics of yours and he'll be able to do it—just like that." The snap of his fingers sounded like a gunshot.

I swallowed past the sudden tightness in my throat. "Mr. Soames?" I asked. At his nod a slow, cold anger coiled itself in the pit of my stomach. "I have ways of dealing with Mr. Soames," I said. "My grand-mother's ways."

I watched as understanding crept into his face. Abruptly, he turned away and began fumbling with his bag. He knows, I thought. At least a part of it.

"You had better be careful," he warned me gruffly. "You are not your grandmother. And Soames isn't a fool, even if he appears to be sometimes."

He sounded tired, defeated, and I thought, *How lonely he must be with Raven gone.* "Will you tell me a little about my grandmother before you go?" I asked hesitantly. "And Rose? No one has told me anything about her."

His expression softened; then the craggy eyebrows drew down and he said sternly, "Only if you promise to think about what I've said."

"I promise," I told him. And I did mean to think about it, though I had no intention of moving from Raven's Rise. I planned to consider very carefully just what I must do to protect myself from Soames and whoever else it was that meant to do me harm. Meanwhile, to lead him away from the subject, I asked, "How could Rose break Raven's heart by leaving her the way she did?"

"Now wait a minute," he said. "Raven wasn't perfect, you know. It's true that she thought the sun rose and set on that girl, but she demanded a lot of her, too. Raven was brought up in the South as a lady, and she couldn't see that it didn't make sense to try and bring her daughter up the same way. Rose was fifteen or so when they got here, and pretty as a picture, and the lads were looking at her, and she was ready to look at them, but Raven wouldn't have it. There weren't any of them good enough." He rubbed a hand across tired eyes. "They looked to be a rough bunch, I'll admit, but some of 'em came from backgrounds every bit as fancy as Raven's. Anyhow, she kept too tight a rein on Rose, I guess, because when Henry Ames came to town, Rose couldn't leave him alone."

"You mean, Rose was the one—"

"Yep. Didn't seem to matter to her that he already had a wife and kids. Not that Henry fought her too hard. His wife was a harpy, as I guess you know, and here was this beautiful young thing throwing herself at him. And what with Will Prentiss sparking her along about then, Raven just wasn't paying attention." He sighed. "So nature took its course. And then, after Rose got—after you were coming along, she was just plain scared to stay here. Raven would've horsewhipped Henry, if she hadn't had him hung, and Rose—I can't even guess what would have happened to Rose. So she did what she thought was best. She followed Henry to San Francisco and let Raven keep her dream of her perfect daughter." He rubbed his eyes again, and this time I realized they held a film of tears. "Poor little girl," he said. "She didn't deserve what happened to her."

For the first time I felt compassion for my mother. I hadn't thought to wonder why she had run off to San Francisco instead of confiding in Raven, nor had it occurred to me how lonely and frightened she must have been. And then, after all that, to have lost her life in such a tragic way.

He patted my arm. "You're getting drowsy. That's good. You just go to sleep and forget about all this."

But I didn't intend to sleep just yet; he had given me too much to think about. My bitter feelings toward my father had lessened somewhat. I had long known that he wasn't a strong-minded man; if he had been, he would not have allowed my foster mother to treat me as she had. Now, though I knew he hadn't the courage to acknowledge me or the moral fiber to resist Rose, I also realized fully how hard it must have been to do as much as he had—to take me in and care for me in the teeth of his wife's disapproval. And he *had* given me love.

I wanted to consider my altered feelings toward Rose and Raven, but sleep overtook me before I had the chance.

I AWOKE FEELING LOGY and dispirited, and when Dulcie pressed me to stay in bed again, I almost did. But as I thought of Dr. Gentry's warning about Soames, that same cold anger stirred in me, and I got up and began to dress. It would suit the banker's purposes very well if I were to hide in my bedroom like a frightened child so he could get control of my house. Then he and his cohorts could search at their leisure for Raven's treasure.

I paused in the act of stepping into my petticoat. It wouldn't be treasure Soames was looking for but the proof that I had found last night! My thoughts raced. In fact, the whole rumor of treasure could have been started by the partners as a way of justifying the frequent break-ins that had occurred since Raven's death.

They would be desperate to find those papers before someone else did, for otherwise the blackmail could go on and on. They hadn't even been sure yesterday, I decided, that I hadn't already known their guilty secret.

I swiftly finished dressing. Even if I were right, it didn't solve the riddle of how they were getting into the house or the problem of how I could put an end to it. But it lifted my burden of fear considerably, for unpleasant as it might be, the thought of Soames or Ogilvey spying on me didn't strike terror into my heart as had that of someone unknown. I went downstairs and surprised Dulcie by eating my breakfast with good appetite.

I didn't, however, venture into the library as yet. Instead, I wandered into the parlor, where I was struck once again by how different it was from the serenity of the rest of the house. I should not have thought Raven's tastes would have run to this plethora of ornaments, no matter how lovely they might individually be. And they were beautiful. I started to pick up one small miniature whose frame was especially ornate but decided against it, for it was covered with dust and tiny cobwebs. Remembering that Dulcie had said Raven took care of this room herself, I decided that I really must get at it soon.

But not today. There were too many things I had to think about, and abruptly I left the parlor.

Dulcie was on her hands and knees in the entry, polishing away the scuffs and dusty footmarks that had marred its usual shine. She stopped working to sit back on her heels and look up at me.

"Mr. Newcomb sure doesn't know his manners, does he? A gentleman doesn't call on a lady that time of night!"

It *had* been late. "I think he was somewhat troubled, Dulcie," I said slowly. "We didn't part on the best of terms." Already I was wishing I hadn't been so defensive yesterday about Raven. Jared had at least been partly right about her, and besides, I increasingly felt the need of a friend. Without realizing it, I sighed deeply.

"You all right, Miss Selina?" The yellow eyes narrowed with speculation. "I can make you a cup of coffee or tea."

"Oh, no, thank you." I tried to speak cheerfully. Dulcie and Hiram seemed to be loyal, but I didn't want to chance a rumor that I was suffering from melancholia. "I plan to do some exploring upstairs. I've scarcely had a chance to look around as yet."

"Want me to go with you? All those empty rooms can give a person a spooky feeling."

So she did think that I had been imagining things. Dr. Gentry was right; I had better take care. I managed to laugh quite normally.

"I've had enough of ghosts and spirits for the time being," I said lightly. "I just want to see the number of rooms and what they are like. If we fall on hard times, we should be prepared to take in boarders." At her scandalized expression I laughed again, quite genuinely this time, and ran upstairs.

But once I reached the upper floor, my facade of gaiety dropped away. There were so many doors, so many silent rooms. Why had Raven built this huge place? Was it a cairn to the love that had died, a futile monument to the world of might-have-been?

I peeked in at a few of the many doors. They opened onto bedrooms that had been furnished in lavish detail, but there was such an unused look about them, such an air of sterility, that I knew they had never been occupied. It saddened me, and I left them and went up the second flight of stairs. To my surprise, a large part of this level was taken up by a spacious ballroom whose polished parquet floor had no doubt never had a dancing footstep mar its glossy perfection. Had Raven stood there, just as I now did, and imagined the room filled with gaiety and laughter? Rose had already been gone for three years when Raven had ordered this built; how had the dream bemused her for so long?

"I wish I could help you," I whispered aloud. "I wish I knew a way to make your dreams come true."

But you can. The thought sprang unbidden to my mind. You can make friends, have balls, even marry and have children to fill some of those empty rooms. If only—if only you can find a way to end the bitterness and hate that is the real legacy of Raven's Rise.

Again guilt and disloyalty plagued me. If I let the three men go free, if I destroyed the papers and told them I had, would it seem that I didn't care that they had ruined the last twenty years of Raven's life? *But I do care, grandmother,* I told her. *It's only that I can't do both. I have to choose between fulfilling your dream and punishing these men for the evil that they did. How am I to know which you would want me to do?*

I waited in the echoing silence of that empty room, but she didn't answer me, and disconsolately I returned to the second floor. As I was passing her bedroom to go to my own, something—some strange compulsion that I couldn't quite identify—caused me to stop before her door. Without willing it, I put out my hand to touch the polished panel, and it swung open as though impelled from within. I drifted into the room.

As though commanded, I went to her bed and dropped to my knees beside it. I lifted the brocade dust ruffle. There, just beneath the edge of the bed, sat a small casket box. It was of polished rosewood, and its curved top had been inlaid with gold in a delicate butterfly design.

I pulled it toward me. Though it was light in weight and didn't feel as though it could contain the purported treasure, my hands shook as I raised its lid.

It was filled with an infant's dainty garments that had yellowed with age. With a sense of wonder, I picked up one and then another to examine them. They were made of cobweb-soft cambric and lawn materials, and each was lovingly embroidered with small, perfect stitches. At first I thought that they must have been Rose's clothing, saved as mementos of her babyhood, but then I remembered Dulcie's tale of their flight from the South and knew that Raven had not brought them with her on that arduous journey.

I continued to lift one garment after another from the chest. Delicate gowns, frilly bonnets, little bibs with graceful sprays of roses, small sacques with matching caps—each embellished with that careful, perfect embroidery. There were even a packet of needles and several skeins of the pastel silk thread, as though the work was not quite done.

I sat back on my heels and considered them. Though they had been made with loving care, they had never been worn.

For what baby had they been sewn?

Tears gathered in my throat. *You knew there was to be a child, grandmother, and that's why you wrote your will the way you did. You never stopped hoping that either Rose or that child would come back to you someday.*

As I replaced the garments carefully in the polished casket, a feeling of happiness came over me, but it was immediately replaced by an overwhelming sense of loss. Raven *would* have welcomed me. Why had my father not risked her anger and brought me home?

Vaguely, I realized that someone had entered the room. I looked up with eyes half blinded with tears to see Dulcie standing beside me. Her face was taut with sympathy.

"She knew about me, didn't she, Dulcie?" I asked. "She made all these in case my mother brought me home."

"She thought Miss Rose was going to have a baby," Dulcie admitted. Her words were heavy with sorrow. "She never knew for sure."

I closed the rosewood lid and touched it gently. "You were there. You knew what was going on. After my mother was killed, why didn't my father bring me home to Raven? Surely he wasn't that afraid of her."

"I just can't say, Miss Selina. Miss Raven never knew about Mr. Henry and Miss Rose, and neither did anyone else until you told us. As far as we knew, Mr. Henry lit out because he was afraid to testify about the gold. If he'd of told the truth, Mr. Soames and his partners would've been after him, and if he'd of lied, Miss Raven would've had a piece of his hide. Nothing had changed by the time you were born, I guess." She knelt beside me and looked earnestly into my face. "Don't you go blaming him too much. Braver men than Mr. Henry would've thought twice about coming back into a mess like that."

I had never stopped to consider my father's actions from other than my own self-centered interests. Now, through Dulcie's words, I could see the past more clearly. If Soames and the others had killed once for gold, they would have done it even more readily to save their own skins. No doubt fearing for his own life if he brought me to Raven, father had done the next best thing: he had taken me into his own home and given me what love and care he had been able to. And remembering my foster mother's unrelenting nature, I thought that he may have been a braver man than any of us gave him credit for.

But any small sympathy I had felt for the three partners had vanished. Whether Raven had known it or not, they had cheated her once more and had robbed me of the maternal love I might have had. An implacable anger filled me. I would make them suffer just as Raven had, but I would find a way to do it without imprisoning myself in the past. I would make them pay and still fulfill her dreams.

Slowly, I became aware that Dulcie had grasped my arms and was speaking urgently to me. "Miss Selina! Are you all right, child? You look to be a million miles away!"

"I'm all right, Dulcie." I pulled away from her and pushed the rosewood box back to its hiding place beneath the bed. "But I would like that coffee now. I have some thinking to do."

CHAPTER THIRTEEN

DULCIE SERVED MY COFFEE in the library after assuring me that Hiram had searched it thoroughly again and, as before, had found nothing.

"It's all right, Dulcie," I said almost impatiently. "I am not worried about it anymore. I was just a little overwrought last night, I'm afraid." I was beginning to think that might have been the case, for I felt no sense of unease at all today.

Dulcie's eyebrows rose, but she went at once to bring my coffee tray. As she left, she muttered something to the effect that "some folks sure are changeable," but I pretended not to hear. In fact, I *did* feel different. It was as though some of Raven's indomitable spirit had entered me so that I might have the strength of mind to carry out whatever course of action I decided on.

I was still sitting beneath Raven's enigmatic gaze when Dulcie announced that Marcus had come to call. Ignoring the leap of excitement in my breast, I told her quite casually to send him in. I did not go to meet him but waited to rise until he had crossed the room with his long, graceful stride.

"How are you, Marcus?" I asked with quiet dignity.

He swept me into his arms and kissed me soundly, and my dignity was forgotten as I responded to the hungry urgency of his lips.

"Much better after that, thank you," he answered. He held me away from him and examined me. "Doc Gentry told me about last night, Selina, and he's right; you do look pale." He smiled and added with a touch of humor, "Beautiful, of course, but decidedly pale." His smile didn't quite reach his hazel eyes.

"I'm perfectly all right." I attempted a return to the quiet dignity. "Will you have coffee?"

"No coffee." The humor had disappeared, and he spoke with an abruptness that was very unlike him. "I would like you to tell me exactly what happened last night."

"It was nothing, really." To avoid meeting his eyes, I turned to look again at Raven's picture. "I thought I could feel someone watching me." Shrugging, I added, "As you can see, with the draperies drawn, that is quite impossible. No doubt it was simply my imagination, as everyone supposed."

There was a silence; then I felt his hand, warm against my shoulder. Gently, he turned me to face him.

"But don't you see, darling, that in either case you shouldn't go on living here?" He felt me stiffen and added, "Please, don't let's quarrel about it, sweetheart. It's only that I love you and don't want you to keep getting upset like this."

"I know." I turned away before the loving concern in his eyes could weaken my resolve. "And I don't enjoy being frightened like that, believe me. But I can't leave just yet." I faced him again, caution shattering in my need for understanding. "There is something unfinished here, Marcus, something that needs doing before Raven can be at peace. She's depending on me. Can't you see that? There's no one else to do it for her."

Again that silence. At last, he said gently, "Yes, I can see that, Selina. Naturally, you have to help her if you can. And I'll help, too, if you'll let me."

Oh, how I wanted him to! I longed to go into his arms again and pour out the whole sad and sordid story. But I could not expect even Marcus to understand Raven's need for revenge and not condemn her. And so I said, "Thank you, dearest. But I'm afraid that I must take care of this myself."

He came closer and began with sudden urgency, "Selina..." Then his tone changed, and he said with his usual gay banter, "If I cannot persuade you to let me help, will you at least go driving with me? It is a beautiful day, and you have been cooped up in this house long enough!" He spoke over my shoulder. "Get Miss Selina's shawl, please, Dulcie. I am taking her out for a breath of air."

"You just do that, Mr. Marcus." Dulcie spoke with heartfelt approval. "A change of scenery will do her a world of good."

"I'd like that, too," I said in smiling agreement. I was so relieved that Marcus hadn't pursued the matter further that I would have agreed to almost anything.

IT DID SEEM GOOD to be out in the open air, and while the sun was hot, the fringed top of the buggy Marcus had procured protected us from the worst of it. He chose a road that led along the river, and the tall spreading trees that grew beside it gave the illusion of coolness. And best of all, we chatted of inconsequential things, and for a time the subject of Raven's Rise wasn't mentioned.

It wasn't until we had traveled some distance from Bittercreek that Marcus pulled up beneath a huge oak that grew on a promontory overlooking the river. Its shade was deep and gave a welcome respite from the afternoon's heat. The horses seemed grateful, too, for they stood with drooping heads and appeared to doze.

"Would you like to get out and stretch a bit?" Marcus asked. When I agreed, he put his hands about my waist and lifted me down, but he didn't let go, nor did I attempt to move away. It seemed so right, so natural, to be sheltered there in his embrace. He bent his head and kissed me—a slow, passionate kiss that left me breathless and with a sweet ache of longing. When he was done at last, I was content to rest my head against his broad chest and enjoy the strength of his encircling arms.

After a while, he released me gently, and we began to stroll toward the riverbank.

"I think you know that I love you, Selina," he began, his voice warm and coaxing, "and I hope that you love me, too. Is it too soon, then, for us to talk a little of the future?" Before I could protest, he added, "I know you feel you have a duty to Raven, but after that is settled? Will you be willing to marry me and come back to San Francisco?"

Startled, I said, "San Francisco? I do want to marry you, but why must we live in San Francisco? You have your business here, and I have Raven's Rise—"

"I have more than one business, dearest, and they are all in San Francisco. I have only held on to the Red Garter out of deference to your grandmother. She never wanted anything in the town to change, and since I loved her, I did what I could to satisfy her wishes. But now that she is gone, I plan to sell the place, or close it permanently. And there is nothing else to bring me back to Bittercreek."

I thought of my vow to make Raven's Rise come to life at last. It was as though I had promised her. "But Marcus—" I turned to face him "—couldn't we— couldn't Bittercreek remain our home? Your businesses seem to run quite well without you, and when you occasionally journey there, I could stay here, in Raven's Rise, with the children—" I blushed a little "—until your return each time."

"My businesses wouldn't continue to run well with that arrangement, I'm afraid. Besides, I have friends there, business acquaintances, a home that needs a woman's touch." He took me into his arms again. "I would want my beautiful wife with me all the time, to share every part of my life. There is nothing for either of us in Bittercreek, Selina. Now that Raven is gone, the town will fade away, as it was meant to do."

He had said the wrong thing. Feeling as though I were being torn from some safe and sheltered nest, I stepped from his arms.

"And then it will be as though she had never lived at all," I said.

He saw his mistake at once.

"I didn't mean that! You are a part of her. As long as your life continues, and yours through your children, she will live, too. Bittercreek is just a town, Raven's Rise just a house, like any other. Why should you attach so much importance to them?"

"I thought you understood," I said accusingly. I felt sick with disappointment and an all-pervading loneliness. "But I realize now that you were just trying to placate me." And then, when he tried to protest again I said, "Please, Marcus, I want to go home."

WE DIDN'T SPEAK AGAIN until he brought me to my door.

"The day I gave you the keys to this house, I warned you against letting it possess you," he said. "But that is just what you are doing." His tone grew urgent. "Please, darling, don't turn your back on life, as Raven did. Say you'll marry me and come to San Francisco."

Suddenly, I didn't want to go back into that huge, lonely house with its dark and terrible secrets. I wanted to throw myself at him, beg him to take me to some place of light and love and laughter where the past, if there was one at all, had no more weight than thistledown.

Then the door opened, and Dulcie stood there, waiting.

BY THE TIME Jared called that evening, I had made my plans. The three men had to be punished, as I had earlier decided, but it must be swift and final. The cat-

and-mouse game that Raven had played with them went totally against my nature. As for Marcus, I could only hope his love would help him see that the course I was taking was the only one open to me.

Even after my bizarre experience in the library the night before, it remained my favorite room, and that is where, in spite of Dulcie's disapproving glances, I entertained Jared.

His usual infectious smile was missing when he greeted me, and the brilliant blue eyes were anxious.

"I have been concerned all day about you," he said. "You seemed so distraught last night, and with nobody to care for you except the servants—"

"No one could care for me better than Dulcie and Hiram." I smiled at Dulcie, who was waiting for further orders. "Will you have coffee, Jared, or would you like a glass of wine?"

"Coffee, please." Ignoring Dulcie, who went out with one last disapproving sniff, he sat in one of the comfortable chairs across from me. "What really happened last night, Selina? I'm a good listener, if you would care to tell me about it."

A little bubble of laughter rose in my throat, the first I had felt for what seemed years. "That I can believe, Jared. I swear your ears grow an inch whenever you suspect a juicy tidbit for your newspaper. But my dreams and nightmares? Surely even the *Bulletin* readers are not interested in them!" I had not forgotten the excuse I had given him last night.

The concern left his mobile face, and he laughed with me, albeit somewhat sheepishly.

"Am I that obvious? I have to admit your accusation has some truth; everything is potential grist for my editorial mill. But that doesn't mean that I'm not truly concerned with your welfare."

He sounded so sincere, and I felt a deep gratitude toward him. "I thank you for that," I said, "and before you leave, I will have a small item that might be of some interest."

"Oh?" The incredible eyes lit up. "Might it have something to do with your future? An announcement, perhaps, of a betrothal?"

I could feel the humor drain from me. "No," I said. "I have no plans for marriage at this time."

There was a small pause.

"What a fool I am," he said quietly. "Forgive me. I just took it for granted that you and Marcus—"

"Marcus's future lies in San Francisco," I said carefully, "while mine is here with Bittercreek and Raven's Rise."

"I see. Then you do plan to make this your permanent home."

There was something—some odd note in his voice—that upset me. I leaped up and began to pace the floor beneath Raven's portrait. "Why should that seem so strange to everyone?" I asked sharply. "That is obviously what she wanted me to do. Why can't anyone see that I really have no choice?"

Jared got up, too. "I didn't mean to upset you. God knows, your happiness is of primary importance to me." He stepped before me to interrupt my pacing and took me by the arms. With a little shock I realized the whipcord strength of his slim body. "Selina, if I thought that with Marcus gone there was a chance for me..."

The blue eyes were blazing with some repressed emotion, and for a moment my pulse quickened in response. Then the feeling died, and sensing it, he let me go. "I'm sorry," he said. "I should have known it is much too soon to bring up such a thing."

"I'm sorry, too. But I have so much on my mind just now. Perhaps someday..." It was a lie to ease the moment, and he knew it, but he seemed grateful for it.

"Of course," he said with a little crooked smile. "Someday. In the meantime, what is this 'juicy tidbit' you have for me?"

Dulcie brought in our coffee, and I waited until she had gone before answering.

"Nothing earthshaking," I said then. "It is simply that I plan a party—actually, a ball, I suppose—to be held here at Raven's Rise two weeks from Saturday night. The entire community is to be invited via your newspaper."

The bushy eyebrows rose, and he whipped out a small notebook and stubby pencil. "A ball. And that date would be—" he calculated rapidly "—the fourteenth." He scribbled furiously for a moment, then looked up and smiled. "Your choice of dates is fortuitous. Senator Bentley will still be in residence at that time."

I felt a small prickle along my spine. "The senator is here in Bittercreek—now?"

"Didn't you know? He arrived this morning. I thought perhaps that was the reason for the ball." He still held the notebook and pencil. "If it isn't, might I know its purpose? If, of course, there is one beyond that of simple pleasure.''

''It is just that I think Raven's Rise has stood empty long enough. It is time for it to come alive, as it was meant to. And it does happen that I plan to make an announcement which will be of interest to the people of the town.''

''An announcement.'' He wrote again, then looked up. ''I suppose I can't hope for a hint of what this announcement will pertain to?''

''Not a hint.'' I gazed serenely at him. ''For once that newsman's curiosity will just have to be content to wait.''

To give him credit, he took me at my word and put the notebook away. As we drank our coffee, we spoke of light and inconsequential things.

I GAVE MUCH THOUGHT to that announcement. I imagined myself to be in the ballroom, standing on the small orchestra stage. I visualized the upturned faces, at first alive with interest and curiosity, changing at my words to shock, disbelief and deep disgust. I saw the fear, the pain, the humiliation in the eyes of the three partners and their families as their neighbors turned their backs to shun them.

I couldn't sleep that night for thinking about it. I told myself over and over that they deserved it, that they should at last be exposed for the greedy murderers that they were. But what about their families, my thoughts whispered. Should they, too, have to bear the burden of disgrace and the cold shouldering of their fellow townspeople? And while the partners themselves had done a terrible thing, at least in the ensuing years they had apparently been decent men, devoted to their families and fellow citizens. I tossed and turned until the bedsheets wound around me like a shroud, but I could not escape the knowledge that I must expose them, that I owed it to my grandmother's memory. My thoughts were in turmoil, and it seemed as though the long, dark night would never end.

But it did end, and with the first pale glow of dawn came a partial solution. I would go ahead with my plan to publicly expose them, but I would call them together and warn them of it first. That way, if they chose to do so, they could gather their families together and leave town, thus avoiding a direct confrontation with neighbors and friends.

Somewhat soothed by this decision, I at last drifted off to sleep and didn't awaken until nearly noon, when Dulcie came to see if I might be ailing.

IMMEDIATELY AFTER my late breakfast and before my resolve could weaken, I dispatched Hiram with notes to Soames, Ogilvey and Senator Bentley. They were stiff little notes, more commands than requests, that the partners call on me at exactly four o'clock. They might be thought presumptuous, as they actually were, but I felt sure that when that time came, the three men would arrive.

At precisely four, the doorbell jingled. I awaited them in the library despite Dulcie's strong feelings on the subject, for I wasn't comfortable in the parlor. Besides, I had not yet dusted it.

Senator Bentley was a tall, attractive, silver-haired man who was, not surprisingly, far more sophisticated and urbane than Ogilvey and Soames. When introduced, he greeted me with just the right mixture of flattery and sincerity. And yet some guardedness of expression, some slight stiffness in his demeanor, indicated a nervousness to match that of the other two.

"Sit down, gentlemen," I said when greetings and introductions were over. "I would offer you refreshments, but this is not a social occasion. Dulcie, I will call you if I need you."

The puzzlement on Dulcie's face deepened to apprehension, but she left the room and closed the door behind her.

"Really, Miss Ames—" Soames was obviously flustered. "I assure you that we are all busy men. We would appreciate it if you would come to the point."

"If you will be seated, I'll do just that." Now that the moment had arrived, I found it difficult to begin, and it didn't help to have the three of them towering over me. Reluctantly, they took the chairs opposite mine, but I didn't immediately join them. Instead, I went to stand before Raven's portrait. *Please, grandmother,* I said silently, *I am doing this for you. Help me to have the courage and the cruelty.*

At last, I turned to face them. Soames's forehead and lips were beading with perspiration. Ogilvey's face had paled to match his cadaverous appearance, and Senator Bentley had taken on the set expression of a man enduring a chronic and debilitating pain. I found it difficult to credit them with cold-blooded, premeditated murder. I steeled myself.

"I don't know why I feel it necessary to warn you," I said, "for certainly you didn't have that compunction in the past. But I have decided you should know that in two weeks' time I intend to announce publicly that in 1851 the three of you murdered Will Prentiss and stole from him the Four Horsemen Mine."

CHAPTER FOURTEEN

THOUGH I WOULD NOT HAVE THOUGHT it possible, Mayor Ogilvey went several shades paler. He sat as though stricken with instantaneous paralysis. Soames, on the other hand, began to quiver from head to foot like a leaf in a thunderstorm. Even his thick jowls shook visibly. It was only Senator Bentley who kept a semblance of poise, though it seemed to me that he aged before my eyes.

The senator struggled slowly to his feet. "You had better be prepared to back up that accusation with proof, young lady, or you will find yourself in very deep trouble." Though he kept his voice low and even, he couldn't quite control a telltale quaver.

"Believe me, senator, I am prepared," I said. "I have found the papers that Raven Winfield had in her possession all these years, and I plan to turn them over to the proper authorities."

Soames tried to speak but couldn't seem to force a sound through his quivering lips. Ogilvey sat on, still in his apparent state of paralysis.

"Why?" the mayor said at last. The words came whispering from between dry lips. "Why are you doing this to us?"

"Why?" I had been finding this singularly unpleasant, but at his words all the bitterness, all the sorrow over Raven's lonely and wasted life, came back to me. "You dare to ask me that? After cold-bloodedly murdering a man in order to rob him of a fortune? I think it is high time you paid, for that and for all the other heartbreak that you caused."

Mr. Soames found his tongue at last. "Pay!" he burst out, his voice high and hysterical. "You talk of pay? We've done nothing *but* pay for the last seventeen years of our lives! And not only with money but with every breath we've drawn! Our lives, our children's—the whole town has been controlled by the vindictiveness of that woman!" He had leapt up as he spoke, and now he pointed one pudgy finger at Raven's smiling portrait. "May she burn in hell for what she did to us!"

I could feel the strength drain from me. I knew then that I had sensed, had feared, had known all along, that Raven had taken some terrible revenge beyond that of money against those who had wronged her. Still, hadn't she had the right? Didn't they, after what they had done, deserve any punishment she could devise?

Rallying, I said as much. "You shot a man and left him to die, then were so little bothered by it that you stole his fortune. What worse thing than that could she have done to you?"

Soames started to speak again, but Senator Bentley cut him off. "Be quiet, Oliver," he ordered in such an authoritative tone that the banker was silenced instantly. "Miss Ames, I can't fault you for thinking as

you do. And maybe we have got off lucky all these
years; certainly we never chose the alternative. But
before you condemn us completely, will you at least let
us tell our side of it and the price we have already
paid?''

I didn't want to hear it. I wanted to go on believing
that Raven had only meted out justice where it was
deserved. But I knew that I had to listen, had to know
the whole story, or I might never sleep again.

"Very well," I said. "But don't think that you will
cause me to change my mind."

For a moment he looked defeated. "If you are
Raven's granddaughter, I would hardly dare to hope.
But for the sake of all of us, I have to try." He rubbed
a hand across his eyes as though thinking where to
begin. "In the first place, we didn't kill Will deliberately. It's true that we followed him that day; we suspected he had struck gold, and according to our
agreement, we were to share and share alike. We didn't
believe that he had found the vein after the partnership broke up. The timing just seemed too convenient. And then, his reason for breaking off with us had
been such a flimsy one. Who cared, we thought at the
time, that Harry, our other partner, had got drunk and
cut off a Chinaman's pigtail? But Will knew, I guess,
how important it was to them, and he and Harry got
into a fight over it. One thing led to another and Will
pulled out."

I remembered reading in the *Bulletin* that the
Chinaman had drowned himself in the creek.

"Anyhow," Senator Bentley went on, "we followed Will that day. I don't know what we planned to

do. Corner him, maybe, make him admit we should share in the strike. Anyhow, he must have realized he was being followed, for the first thing we knew he was shooting at us. A couple of us shot back.''

Bentley stopped speaking then, and his eyes went to Soames.

"Don't look at me like that!'' Soames said sharply. "You know it was Harry's bullet that got him! I never could hit the broad side of a barn!''

"Harry was drunk, as usual,'' the senator said levelly, "so we don't know for sure. But whoever did it, we were all guilty. When we saw that Will was unconscious, we thought maybe he hadn't recognized us, so we decided to put him in that cabin and get Doc Gentry.'' It seemed to me that the lines in his face deepened as he recalled the events of that long-ago time. "We drew straws to see who would leave a note on Doc's door, and Harry got the short one. But I guess Doc never got the note, because he didn't go to the cabin, and Will died.''

They were all silent then, as though burdened with the guilt of years. At last I ventured, "What did Dr. Gentry say about it?''

"We couldn't ask him.'' Mayor Ogilvey's voice sounded old and querulous. "That would've been putting our necks right in the noose.''

"And you see, Harry—'' Senator Bentley said, "Harry was so drunk by then that he never could remember if he had actually delivered the note or not.'' He cleared his throat. "I think it was the not knowing that got to him. He died of drink not more than a year later.''

His story told, the senator sat down again, and they looked at me as I imagine the accused in a courtroom looks at the jury that is to pass judgment on them. And I felt the same weight that jury might feel. For if I believed their story, they had not been the cold-blooded murderers I had thought them but merely hotheaded young men who acted on impulse and then had had a natural desire to save their own skins.

I hardened myself against the stirrings of pity.

"Nevertheless," I accused them, "you acted in a greedy, cowardly manner. If you had been men enough, Will Prentiss might be alive today.

Surprisingly, it was Soames who spoke up this time. "Don't you think we know that?" It was as though the words came grinding out of some deep, painful recess of his soul. "Don't you think we know what it is to live with that all these years?"

"Then—" I groped for words "—why do you blame Raven for avenging him?"

In answer, Senator Bentley took up the story again.

"When Raven came to us two years later and told us she had found Will's papers, we offered her his share of the profits. We still didn't know, don't know yet, whether he had been cheating us or not, but we felt bad enough about his death to give her that. But that was too easy on us, she said. Not only did she want the money, but she told us that she was going to make us stay in this town for the rest of our lives, just as we had made Will stay here. And she built this house overlooking the town so that we would be reminded every day of our lives of what we had done."

A silence fell; then Mayor Ogilvey broke it by adding sadly, "Here we were, with more money than a man ever dreams of, and we couldn't go anywhere to spend it. Even Bentley here had to ask her permission before he could run for senator."

"She graciously gave it," the senator said dryly, "provided that this remain my official home and that I reside here whenever the senate isn't in session."

"But the worst of it was our families," Soames said. He had begun to tremble again, and sweat was running down his jowls. "We had to make them stay here, too, you know. How would you like to have to tell your son that if he moves away he might be the cause of his father hanging for murder? Oh, she owned us, all right, and our families, and through us, the whole danged town!"

I felt a quiver start deep inside me as at last I saw with shocking clarity the awful price that Raven had exacted. These were the three most important men in the town, and she had held them in the palm of her hand. No wonder that no business flourished without her approval, no loans were granted, no licenses issued. I felt faint with the enormity of it.

"I'm surprised," I said, "that you weren't tempted to...do away with her."

Their silence spoke for them.

"I won't say we didn't think of it," the senator said at last. "But we aren't murderers. We are trying to tell you that." He didn't add that without knowing where the papers were, they hadn't dared to act, but the fact hung almost palpably in the air.

I went again to look into Raven's smiling face. *I'm sorry, grandmother*, I said silently, *but I can't do it. What you hoped to gain by exacting such a terrible price I may never know, but it has to end now. Please forgive me if it isn't what you would have had me do.*

When I turned to face the three partners, they had risen, too, and were waiting with the expressions of mingled dread and apprehension. I went to the cupboard beneath the bookcases, and kneeling before it, opened the secret panel. As I brought out the oilskin packet, I heard a stir behind me and a slight moan that seemed to come from Mr. Soames.

"These are the papers, gentlemen," I said as I returned to them. "A map of the strike, the assayer's report and a letter to Raven from Will Prentiss. They might not convict you, but they are certainly incriminating."

No one spoke, but three pairs of eyes watched with the desperate look of caged animals who could see the chance of freedom at last. As I picked up a fireplace match, I said, "I don't know why my grandmother did what she did, but it seems to me that by now you have all paid quite enough." I struck the match and held it to the papers. They caught immediately, and when they were blazing well, I dropped the flaming remains into the fireplace.

When the last bit of paper had been consumed, Senator Bentley said with some difficulty, "To say 'thank you' is totally inadequate. You have given us back our freedom."

"If not our money," Mr. Soames said.

"Stow it, Oliver!" Mayor Ogilvey said sharply. The parchment color of his countenance had returned to a normal pink tinge. "That was Will's share. For all we know, the whole blasted mine belonged to him, so be happy this little lady is leaving you any part of it!"

My heart sank further.

"Then my...Raven did actually demand payment from you." I had not wanted to believe she had gone so far as that.

"Every month!" Soames sounded disgruntled in spite of the mayor's warning. "We had to sit in that parlor and drink tea with her while she robbed us blind!"

"I'm sorry," I said slowly. "I don't know where that money is. The funds in the estate have been well accounted for."

"Forget about the money, Miss Ames." Senator Bentley spoke in his most authoritative manner. "And you, too, Soames. There's no telling what she did with it. As far as Ogilvey and I are concerned, it never existed." He held out his hand to me. "Thanks to you, I can now get on with my life. I only hope that you will do the same."

"That is exactly what I intend to do," I said.

But after I had rung for Dulcie to see them out and was alone again, I felt suddenly bereft. Who was this smiling woman in the portrait, actually? Was she the loving, caring, tender woman I had thought her, the woman to whom Marcus and Dr. Gentry had long been devoted? Or was she the vindictive, heartless harridan she had seemed to those who had been in her power?

"If only I could believe you had a reason," I said aloud. "If only I knew that it wasn't just for money or power, or even revenge. I think I wouldn't feel as though I had lost you, then."

But I did feel it, and I had a sudden longing for Marcus. Perhaps he would think differently about living in Bittercreek if he knew that I no longer had a "vendetta," as he had called it, against the town. And it was true; my need for revenge was gone, and I felt as though a great weight had been lifted from me. There only remained my promise to Raven—that I would make Raven's Rise come to life and fulfill her dream for it. But how was I to do that unless I could persuade Marcus to live there with me? I had already seen in those few moments with Jared that no one else would ever be able to take Marcus's place in my heart.

Impulsively, I summoned Dulcie.

"Please have Hiram leave messages at the Red Garter and at the hotel that I would like to see Mr. Hannaford as soon as it is convenient for him," I told her.

Her eyes widened, and a slow grin spread across her face. "Yes, ma'am!" she answered, and then added, "You want me to hold dinner for a while?"

There was very little that Dulcie missed. "For a while," I conceded. "Until Hiram returns, at least."

He was back in a very few minutes. At my expectant glance, he shook his head. "He weren't at neither place, Miss Selina. But I left the message. He be along soon, I reckon."

But he didn't come, and eventually I gave in to Dulcie's persuasion and ate a few bites of dinner, then returned to the library. I tried to recapture the feeling of release that had come to me earlier, tried to revel in the knowledge that Raven's Rise was truly mine at last, that all reason for fear and nighttime terrors had been removed with my act of burning those incriminating papers, but it didn't seem to matter at the moment. I couldn't settle down. I paced the library, then tried sampling several of the pristine volumes from the bookshelves, but each seemed incredibly boring. And with my impatience came a growing feeling of unease. It was almost as though I could again sense alien eyes watching from the shadows of this room. I knew it was nonsense, but the feeling persisted, and I called for Dulcie to close the draperies and light every lamp. While she was with me, I felt reassured, but no sooner had she gone than the unpleasant sensation returned. I tried to ignore it but at last put down the latest book, of which I had comprehended not one word, and went into the hall.

"Dulcie, I am going out," I called, and without waiting for her answer, snatched my shawl from its hook and went outside.

I went down the walk and slipped through the iron gates; then I stood in the shadows of the oaks and regarded the dark bulk of Raven's Rise. For the first time I accepted the fact that I would have to leave it. I saw now that I had allowed it, and Raven, to become an obsession, just as Marcus had feared. I could only hope for a chance to convince him that I had, at last, put the past behind me.

As I reached the hotel, I carefully skirted the pool of light that fell from the open doorway. I suppose I was secretly hoping to encounter Marcus, but pride wouldn't let me openly seek him out. I could only stand in the shadows near Jared's darkened office and stare wistfully across at the Red Garter Saloon, from which came lights and gay music and an occasional burst of raucous laughter.

Reluctantly, I turned homeward. Soon I stood again before the mansion. It seemed to loom over me as much as it had that first night in Bittercreek, when I had felt so strangely drawn to it and yet repelled.

It was growing late; the night was beginning to lose its warmth, yet I remained in the shadows before the house. I was loath to go in, for I dreaded a return of that chilling sense of an alien presence, even though, or perhaps especially because, I knew now that it was simply my imagination. But at last I sighed with resignation and started to move from beneath the sheltering trees.

It was then that I saw the unmistakable glimmer of a tiny light, just as I had seen it twice before. Only this time it came not from the library, whose draperies were closed, but from one of the smaller windows on the third floor.

CHAPTER FIFTEEN

I STOOD TRANSFIXED as the light flickered once, then disappeared. I did not imagine it, I thought stubbornly. Someone must be in the house, searching yet again for a thing that must be of incredible importance to him. It couldn't be any of the three partners searching for the papers, for they knew the necessity was gone. Either someone else suspected the evidence of those papers and didn't know they had been destroyed, or—

Knowledge flooded me. The papers had never been the object of those searches. Someone—the someone who was upstairs in my house right now—must be totally convinced that the rumored treasure did exist, and he was prepared to go to any length to find it.

As the light shone briefly once again, a slow burning anger suffused me. This—this *being* who prowled so boldly through my home had caused me anguish and terror from the first night I had occupied it, had lost me the only love I had ever had, had even, with deliberate aforethought, made me doubt my own sanity. I simply could not allow him to get away with it.

Upon the thought, I sped up the walk to the porch. The front door was unlatched as I had left it, and I slipped inside and closed it silently. By the light of the lamp that still burned brightly on the hall table, I ran to the servants' bedroom.

"Dulcie! Hiram!" I hissed the words through their closed door. "Come quickly! Someone is in the attic!"

I had hardly got the words out of my mouth before Hiram flung open the door. He had obviously just pulled on his trousers, and his suspenders were hanging untidily at his hips. Dulcie peered over his shoulder with widened eyes.

"I saw the light," I whispered swiftly "when I was outside just now. Oh, Hiram, there really is somebody! Can't we trap him somehow?"

There was nothing slow about his thought processes or his movements.

"The stairs," he said, speaking more rapidly than I had ever heard him before. "I'll get the back ones. You and Dulcie get to the front. Ain't no other way out of this place." With that he was off down the hall, hauling his suspenders over his shoulders, his bare feet slipping on the polished floor.

Dulcie was equally swift. She turned back into her bedroom and with one sweep grabbed the two heavy brass candlesticks that stood on her dresser. She handed one to me, and we ran together toward the front hall. When we had passed the stairway's beginning, she flattened herself in the shadows of the parlor door and motioned for me to do the same on the library side.

Candlesticks at the ready, we stood thus for several minutes, neither of us visible from or able to see the stairway.

There was no sound from upstairs, or indeed from anywhere at all. The whole house was utterly silent. I began to think that if I didn't hear *something* soon, I would go mad, for it was as though I had been suddenly stricken deaf.

I got my wish. The doorbell jingled shockingly in the silence, stretching my taut nerves unbearably. I jumped and let out a piercing scream, and Dulcie promptly followed my example. Immediately, the unlocked door swung open, and Marcus burst in. Astonishment spread over his face as Dulcie and I, our candlesticks raised in an involuntary reflex, confronted him, and Hiram came pounding toward us from the rear of the house.

"What—!" Marcus said, and it was exclamation and question in one.

I quickly lowered my weapon.

"Someone is in the attic," I said rapidly. "I'll send Hiram up the back way."

Making no attempt at stealth, Marcus took the steps three at a time, but the noise of his going would make no difference now. Our shrieks could have been heard by the intruder in the farthest reaches of the house.

Dulcie ran to intercept Hiram, and together they ran back the way he had come. Over her shoulder she called to me, "Don't try to stop him, Miss Selina! All we need is to know who he is."

Though I nodded reassuringly, I took a fresh grip on the candlestick. If the intruder thought to escape this way, he might find it more difficult than he had bargained for.

But after what seemed forever, it was only Marcus who came down those stairs. He shook his head in answer to my inquiring look.

"I'm sorry, Selina. We couldn't find a trace of anyone."

"But he must be there! Hiram says there is no other way out than down the two staircases."

"We looked everywhere. On both floors we searched out every cranny big enough for a man to hide in and a lot of them that weren't. Either there is another way out, or he simply vanished into thin air."

My excitement had receded with the long nerve-racking wait, and all that remained was a dull, burning anger.

"But he *was* there," I said slowly. I could feel color flame along my cheekbones. "You do believe that, don't you?"

I thought Marcus waited just a moment too long before he answered. "Of course I believe it. I wish we could have found some evidence of it, though."

"I see." Pride stiffened my spine. "Thank you for your help, Mr. Hannaford, but I think you had better go now."

Instead, he came to me. "Why do you keep sending me away?" He ran the back of his fingers lightly down my cheek. "Don't you know we are meant for each other?"

Oh, how I wanted to believe it, wanted to throw myself into his arms and beg him to take me with him to whatever safe and sheltered place he was going. But pride would not let me melt into the arms of a man who seemed to think me mad.

"Once I thought so," I returned. "But it is obvious that you don't believe in me. And a marriage without trust or faith wouldn't really be a marriage at all."

A wry smile curved his lips. "You are quite right," he said softly. "But remember that faith must come from both parties." He bent his head and kissed me lightly, then went out into the night.

It took all of my will not to go running after him.

AFTER I HAD REVEALED my suspicions about the treasure to Dulcie and Hiram, they both swore they didn't know anything about it. But they did profess to believe me and offered to help in any way they could.

"We will have to go over every room in the house very carefully," I told them. "It might be in a chest with a false back or behind a loose brick in one of the chimneys or—" I thought of the sliding panel in the bookcase "—perhaps under a loose floorboard or a piece of wall paneling. Or even beneath one of the beds. I know a hundred treasures would fit under mine."

"But that's like looking for a needle in a haystack!" Dulcie protested. "Especially when we don't even know what kind of thing we're looking *for*."

"It could be in the form of money or gold or even precious jewels, I suppose." The thought of stumbling across such a thing seemed to be more improbable as we talked. "Or even," I reminded her, "there may be no treasure. After all, we are only supposing that is what someone is looking for." I hadn't mentioned the blackmail. If they didn't suspect, I meant them to keep their illusions about Raven.

Dulcie said quietly, "Do *you* really believe there's a treasure, Miss Selina?"

I thought of all the years Raven had been collecting the money. "Yes, I do believe it, Dulcie. And so does someone else. And he won't stop looking for it until he knows that it has been found."

"I'd like to find *him*," Hiram muttered darkly. "Ain't right to go scarin' folks the way he done."

"You two seem to believe me, at least. That means a lot, you know."

They exchanged glances. Then Dulcie said, "We heard things before you came. Only—"

"Only we thought it really was a ghost. An' at first we thought you was seein' her, too."

I realized then that they hadn't been uneasy because they thought I was imagining things, but quite the opposite. I said, "If it was Miss Raven's spirit, there wouldn't be anything to fear. She would love you just as much as ever." Then I added, with an attempt at gaiety, "But let's get busy. We have a treasure to find!"

BUT WE DIDN'T FIND IT, and the more we searched, the more monumental the task seemed to become. Fortunately, the attic spaces were nearly bare, for Raven had discarded very little over the years. There were only a couple of trunks partly filled with outdated clothing, and these yielded no hidden areas or false bottoms. The ballroom we searched carefully because of its many mirrors and carved wooden panels behind which secret niches could have been built, but I didn't really expect to find anything there. Nor was I surprised when the many spare bedrooms yielded nothing. I was convinced that because of its very nature, and because of *her* nature, the treasure would be found where Raven spent most of her time, for she would have wanted to reassure herself often that it was still safe. I felt that for her it was a symbol of her vindication of Will's death and therefore, if it existed at all, would be found in her bedroom or in the more often used rooms downstairs.

The library was my first choice and the most tedious to search. I insisted that each volume be taken out and examined, for I had often read in mystery stories of books being hollowed out and used for hiding places, but they yielded nothing beyond corroboration of my suspicions that Raven had not been an avid reader. The shelves themselves were also gone over carefully, and I showed the two servants the movable panel as an example of what they might expect to find. Neither of them had suspected that such a thing existed.

"Wasn't Miss Raven a clever one, though!" Dulcie exclaimed in admiration. "She must of planned all that out herself in case she wanted to hide something. Old Mr. Peabody would never of thought of it."

I felt a ray of hope. "Mr. Peabody was the builder? Then perhaps he would remember another such niche. Does he still live in Bittercreek?"

"He died about three years ago," Dulcie said. "He gave her the plans, and she burned 'em. I remember that. Said Raven's Rise was unique, and she never wanted another built like it." Dulcie put her hands on her hips and looked at the shambles we had made of the library. "Right now I wish she *hadn't* been so clever. What good is a treasure if nobody can find it?"

I had to agree, and search as we might, it seemed as though nobody *was* going to be able to find it. If it existed at all.

At last I called a halt. We had been looking for days, and the initial excitement had long worn off. We had thought of nothing else, talked of nothing else and except for those times when Hiram had, of necessity, hurried to the general store for supplies, not one of us had even stepped outside. We were sated with searching, and I had grown so jaded by it that I found myself doubting that we would recognize the treasure if it were suddenly to be dangled right before our eyes.

"Let's just forget it for a while," I told the tired pair. "Perhaps we are trying too hard. After all, if grandmother wants me to have it, surely she will find a way to let me know where it is."

Seeing the alarm in Dulcie's eyes, I immediately regretted the remark, but I hadn't been wholly jesting. Though I wouldn't have admitted it to Marcus, I could not quite believe that all those times I had felt her presence had been caused by my too vivid imagination.

I wandered into the parlor, which I had gingerly searched alone in deference to Raven's hodgepodge of ornaments. I seemed to avoid the library now, though it was where I had sensed her presence most strongly, for ever since I had given her enemies their freedom, the eyes in the portrait had appeared to look at me more with accusation than love.

I didn't really believe that one could talk to spirits, but I also didn't rule out the possibility that they existed. So, feeling more than slightly foolish, I went into the cluttered parlor and sat in the chair that had been Raven's. I was tired, and I leaned my head against its high, curved back and closed my eyes. My thoughts kept returning to our searches. It was, as Dulcie had said, like looking for a needle in a haystack. If Raven wanted the treasure found, I thought almost with annoyance, why hadn't she left some word? A note, perhaps, tucked into one of the desk drawers or a clue scribbled cryptically in the flyleaf of a book. Or even a map glued carefully to the bottom of a drawer. But we had thought of all those things, and there had not been found so much as a hint of treasure. And as Dulcie had also said, what good was a treasure if nobody could ever find it?

No good at all.

I shut my eyes again. The incriminating papers had been hidden cleverly enough, but Raven had not intended that they should ever be discovered. Whereas she surely would have wanted any treasure she had amassed to be found by her rightful heirs. But how did one half hide something? Either one must hide the thing completely or disguise it and—

My heart gave a sudden jolt. A hot tingling sensation ran clear to my fingers and down to the tips of my toes. Slowly, with childlike wonder, I opened my eyes.

And leave it right out in plain sight.

CHAPTER SIXTEEN

I DIDN'T TELL ANYONE about the treasure. It was so obvious, so highly visible, that I scarcely dared think of it myself for fear that I might communicate its whereabouts to others. I didn't want it touched until I had decided what I must do about it.

By its very placement it seemed to give me greater insight into Raven's nature, and I did not at all like what I perceived. For I saw with overwhelming clarity that in this cluttered room she had entertained the three partners with malicious delight. Not only had they been forced to pay tribute, but unbeknownst to them, the painful and humiliating experience had taken place in the very presence of that which their tribute had bought.

The enormity of Raven's bitterness and hatred was brought home to me at last, shattering all of my remaining illusions concerning both her and Raven's Rise. I had already decided that I must leave here, but now that didn't seem drastic enough. I felt that the mansion's walls must be permeated with the wickedness of her thoughts and actions over the years and that the miasma she had produced had reached out and enveloped the whole town.

After brooding about it for some time, it came to me that the only way to disperse that dark and vaporous poison was to remove the sullen presence from which it came. I resolved that the day I left Bittercreek, Raven's Rise would be razed to the ground.

But what about the treasure? I wanted no part of it, yet I would not return it to the three partners, for it would be like rewarding them for their part in bringing evil to the town. I thought at last of setting up some sort of fund to be used for charitable purposes once I had returned to San Francisco.

It took many lonely and troubled hours to reach these decisions, but once I had, a lightness of spirit came over me such as I had never experienced. When I left Raven's Rise, I would be really free for the first time, for the money left to me from what I considered to be Raven's legitimate investments was enough to keep me from want for the rest of my life. The only clouds that still hung over me were my disappointment and sense of loss because I could no longer venerate my grandmother, and my aching desire for Marcus Hannaford.

I had been too rash in my behavior toward him; I realized that now. He had warned me from the beginning not to let this house possess me, and not only had I done that, but I had apparently created out of thin air the sweet and loving presence I had felt within it simply because I had desired it so strongly. Marcus loved me, and he had no doubt sensed the danger because of that love, but I had been too headstrong and willful to heed his warnings. Now perhaps it was too late.

I hastily put that last thought from me. It could not be too late. As he had said, we were meant for each other. I decided that I would send Hiram to him with an invitation to dine with me; when he arrived, I would apologize and explain as best I could.

But what if he had grown weary of my capricious behavior and refused to come? How, then, could I tell him of my change of heart?

I could think of only one way he would be sure to learn of it. He must read of my plans for the future in the *Bittercreek Bulletin*.

JARED ARRIVED PROMPTLY in answer to my note of invitation. A smile of pleasure lit his face as he greeted me, and to my immense relief it was as though there had never been that moment when he indicated that he cared for me. He had befriended me, and it would have upset me to feel that I had hurt him.

"I think it is time I kept my promise to you," I began after we had gone into the library. "I told you that you would be the first to know if I had news of any importance. And now I have."

He took out his notebook and waited expectantly. "And that is?" he queried as my silence lengthened.

I had not dreamed how hard it would be to put it into words. "Oh, Jared," I said, "it's such a big decision. I almost..." I hesitated, then plunged on with determination. "I am leaving Bittercreek—permanently. And when I go, I will give orders for Raven's Rise to be torn to the ground."

For once, Jared's gay smile disappeared. His blue eyes seemed to darken, and I realized that the pupils had grown large, as though with shock.

"But why?" He glanced around as though visualizing the destruction. "I thought you loved this house, Selina."

"I did love it. But it has known too much unhappiness." I rose and went to stand before Raven's portrait, a thing I hadn't done since finding the treasure. "Do you think that houses can take on the personalities of the people who live in them?"

"It's possible, I suppose. And you are right; your grandmother was a very unhappy woman. I felt it the few times I came to visit her. But does that mean you must tear down the house she loved? It seems to me to be a terrible waste."

I turned from the painting. "You said once that the townspeople feared her. If that is so, then perhaps when Raven's Rise is torn down, the past will be forgotten."

"You no doubt have learned a great deal about Raven, living here," Jared said. "Did you ever find out why they feared her?" His tone was uninterested, almost idle, but I felt a sudden note of warning. He might be my friend, but he was first and foremost a newspaperman. I had better take care not to let him guess any part of the truth.

"I suppose because she was so rich." I shrugged elaborately. "People have always been jealous of those who have more than they."

"Especially when they seem to do so little to earn it." He glanced again at the rich brocades, the heavily carved furniture, the wealth of books that lined the walls. "I confess that to have a room like this would fulfill my highest ambition. Apparently Raven left you a great deal if you can give it up without a pang."

I thought of the fortune waiting in the parlor and felt my face grow warm.

"Enough for my needs, certainly," I said evasively. "I'm not so sure having money brings all the pleasure I thought it would."

The infectious grin returned, but the eyes were shrewd. I felt that he could read my guilty secret and was relieved when he merely said, "I'd like to judge that firsthand someday. But for the moment I had better attend to my editorial duties, else even that modest income will be denied me. Tell me, does this mean that the ball has been canceled?"

I had scarcely thought of the ball from the day I had told Jared of it, since its purpose, that of exposing the three men, was gone. I had, I suppose, simply assumed that I would cancel it. But some hint of criticism in Jared's question brought me up sharply.

"That would disappoint a lot of people, wouldn't it?" I said slowly. "I don't suppose many of them have been inside Raven's Rise, and if it is to be torn down, this will be their last chance. No, report that the ball is to be held as planned, even though I am leaving Bittercreek directly after."

He asked me several more questions, most of which I couldn't answer, as they were about my future plans, then put his notebook and pencil away.

"I think that when all this is over, I'll close the *Bulletin* and move on myself," he said. His usual lightheartedness was gone. "Without Raven's Rise to set it apart, Bittercreek will be nothing at all."

I murmured some appropriate words of surprise and protest at his decision, but I was beset by guilt. Not only was I failing to keep my promise to Raven, but I was influencing Jared's life and creating havoc in heaven knew how many others. I closed my eyes against the thought.

"I must be going, Selina." I opened my eyes again at Jared's words. He had risen and was standing near me. "This has no doubt been a difficult decision for you. I won't keep you from your dinner and an early night's rest."

Though I wasn't really tired, I didn't protest his leaving, for I wanted to send Hiram in search of Marcus.

BUT AS HAD HAPPENED once before, Marcus was nowhere to be found. At last, at Dulcie's urging, I forced down a little of her delicious dinner, but my thoughts were bitter. What had been the use, after all, of my coming to Bittercreek? Granted, my financial future was secured, but I still faced the loneliness, the lack of family and emotional ties, with which I had always been plagued. Perhaps, I thought with self-disgust, I didn't deserve them. Hadn't my obstinacy and self-will driven Marcus away when he had offered me more than I had ever dreamed of possessing?

After dinner I wandered disconsolately through the empty rooms, remembering how I had once longed to do this very thing. I had thought then that possessing Raven's Rise and all that went with it would give me joy, but it had only brought sorrow and an aching sense of loss. Marcus hadn't wanted me to move into the mansion, had repeatedly cautioned me that to do so would mean unhappiness and danger. He hadn't even been willing to concede that I was Raven's inheritor until faced with the incontestable evidence of the emerald ring.

My thoughts stopped at that. It had surprised me at the time, for I would have thought him predisposed to believe me, considering the interest he had already begun to show. I remembered how solicitous he had been when I had fainted in the parlor and of his concern when I had revived and then had nearly swooned again at the sight of yet another portrait showing the emerald ring—my ring—on Raven's finger. When he had turned with sudden alertness to look at it, I had feared that he suspected the reason for my agitation.

I dwelled on that moment with a growing sense of unease. I could remember his face exactly, and in retrospect I recognized his expression was that of dawning comprehension. I was certain now that he had realized a connection between my fainting and my viewing of Raven's portrait. But if that were so, why had he been adamant in his disavowal of my claim to Raven's Rise?

I moved restlessly about the room. Something was troubling me, some thought that lay just below the surface of my mind. It was true that in being cautious Marcus had only been dutiful to his position as executor of Raven's estate, but wasn't it as much his duty to *find* an heir as it was to refute impostors? Yet he had not really considered my claim until I had presented the irrefutable evidence of the ring.

Had Marcus not *wanted* me to inherit Raven's Rise? Perhaps my living in the house might interfere with plans of his own.

I felt jolted as though by an earthquake tremor. No, not Marcus! He couldn't have perpetrated the cruel, abominable trick of trying to convince me I was losing my mind. It was simply because of his love for me that he had urged me to go to a place of safety.

I had only partially convinced myself of his innocence when I heard a sudden commotion in the hall. Dulcie was protesting in a shocked voice, "Hiram, have you gone crazy? Why for you pointing that shotgun at Mr. Marcus?"

Icy lead hit the pit of my stomach, and I began shaking as though with the ague. I could stand only by supporting myself with the back of a tall chair, and I was waiting rigidly there as Hiram, ignoring his agitated wife, herded Marcus unceremoniously in to confront me.

"Selina," Marcus said, and his tone was a mixture of embarrassment and annoyance, "will you tell Hiram that it is all right to point that blunderbuss elsewhere? One slip of his trigger finger and I'll be sporting a hole you could put a cannon through."

I felt incapable of speech. I knew the color was draining from my face, and the alarm that sprang to Marcus's eyes confirmed it. He started toward me but was stopped by a gesture of Hiram's shotgun.

"Sorry, Mr. Marcus," Hiram said firmly, "but you got to stay away from Miss Selina till she hears what happened."

"Then you go to her, Dulcie," Marcus commanded. "Can't you see she is about to faint?"

I found my voice. "It's all right, Dulcie. I am not going to faint. Hiram, I know you must have good reason for what you are doing. Please tell me what it is."

Now that the moment had arrived, Hiram seemed not so sure of himself. He shuffled his feet a moment before he said slowly, "I knowed Mr. Marcus a long time, and I know he was Miss Raven's friend. But I got to protect you now, Miss Selina. I just want Mr. Marcus to tell you why he was tryin' to get in one of the basement windows."

A slow pounding began in my temples. Marcus. Marcus whispering my name in that evil manner, Marcus spying on me from some unknown spot, Marcus trying to get me to leave Raven's Rise so he could continue to prowl the house in search of treasure without interference. Marcus, whose avowal of love was just another ruse to get me out of the way. I closed my eyes and felt a slow trickle of tears slide down my cheeks.

"I see you have me tried and found guilty on just that evidence," Marcus said quietly. "Where is the faith we spoke of once before?"

I lifted my head proudly. "We spoke of many things, such as love and caring and marriage. But I have forgotten them now." His beloved face was blurring through my tears. "I only remember fear and loneliness and the terror of thinking I was losing my mind.''

"Selina, I am not responsible for those things! I was only trying to discover how he has been getting in! Dear girl, why won't you just this once allow yourself to trust your heart?''

"I have no heart," I answered in a hard voice. "I gave it to someone, and he threw it away. Which is just as well, for the judgment of hearts is very unreliable. Hiram, please take Mr. Hannaford to the sheriff and have him locked up. I plan to press charges against him.''

There was a moment's silence; then Hiram moved forward and gestured with the shotgun. "Sorry, Mr. Marcus," he said again. "I can't think you was doin' wrong, but I dassn't take no chances with Miss Selina's safety.''

Marcus didn't take his eyes from me. "Quite right," he said, "for she is in danger. That's why I have been guarding the house. But he has been slipping by me, and tonight I was trying to determine just how.''

I hardened my heart against him. "A very good story," I said coldly, "but hardly believable." I turned my back. "Please, Hiram, take him away *now*.''

There was a silence after they had gone, and I thought I was alone. I had forgotten Dulcie.

"Mmm, mmm," she said. "It's hard to say who's the bigger fool, you or Hiram.''

Shocked, I swung to face her. Gone was the servant's bland, innocuous expression. The look she gave me was a combination of anger, disgust and something very near to contempt.

"How dare you!" I exclaimed furiously. "It is not your place—"

"I don't *have* a place," she said. "I may be colored, but I'm free, and I got money in the bank, thanks to Miss Raven. And it's because of her that I'm standing here telling you that you're a fool, thinking what you are about Mr. Marcus. Why would he do all those things you say he did?"

"Why, so he could look for the treasure," I answered defensively. "He knew her well. He must be really convinced there is one."

Her look of disgust deepened. "Mr. Marcus is executor of the estate. It's been nearly six months since she died, and he could of come in every single day to search if he thought there was something hidden here. There wasn't no need for him to come sneaking around with a little firefly light to try and find it."

I had not thought of that. "Yes, but then he would have had to declare it as part of the estate! And he didn't want that. He wanted it for himself."

She made a sound of annoyance. "You think he isn't smart enough to figure a way to sneak it out of here if he wanted to? Nobody was paying any attention. Everybody in the town trusts Mr. Marcus; don't you know that? Besides, he has made more money already than he knows what to do with. Why would he want to go crawling around at night looking for more?"

I was speechless. Every word she had said was true; I knew it in the depths of my being. And I knew, too, that I had done it again; I had taken my chance of happiness and destroyed it because of my stubborn and suspicious nature. It wasn't by chance that I had not considered Marcus's unlimited access to the house; after all, I had figured out Raven's much more complicated past. No, it was because deep in my heart I had to think he had had an ulterior motive for courting me. I was afraid to believe that anyone could love me for myself, for to do so would render me vulnerable to hurt, and I dared not cast off the protective shell I had always worn against it.

I felt the tears stream down my cheeks. "Oh, Dulcie!" I said. "You're right! And Marcus will never forgive me."

"He'll forgive you." Dulcie shook her turbaned head, apparently at my obtuseness. "Don't you know anything about love, child? He'll forgive you ten times over if need be. But to my mind he'll forgive you a lot faster if you don't let him spend too much time in that jail."

I gasped. "What shall I do? Quick, fetch my shawl. I'll have to go to the sheriff's office right away!"

She was grinning now. "Don't fret yourself. I'll go after them. The mistress of Raven's Rise can't go running through the streets after any man." Before I could argue with her, she was gone.

At first I paced about, praying silently that Marcus would actually be willing to give me one more chance; then, as time passed and they hadn't returned, my agitation abated somewhat. I again took the chair before Raven's portrait. Our eyes met and locked, and for long moments we gazed at each other until at last I seemed to read her very thoughts.

"I think I understand now, grandmother," I said slowly. "It wasn't you who needed me all this time. It was I who needed you. I have been reaching out to you, clinging to your memory, because I wanted so badly to belong to someone. And yet when Marcus offered me love, I was afraid to risk it." I closed my eyes, visualizing his dear face. Then my mood changed abruptly, and I exclaimed impatiently, "Oh, Dulcie, hurry! What can be taking so long!"

It was then that I heard a creaking sound and a small, oddly familiar chuckle. As I glanced toward the sound, I could feel the blood congealing in my veins, for a portion of the bookcases was slowly swinging inward.

CHAPTER SEVENTEEN

JARED STOOD THERE, wearing his funny, crooked smile.

I couldn't at once credit my senses, couldn't grasp the significance of his appearing like an apparition from the very walls of my house. I got no further than an astounded "Jared!" when he stepped toward me from the narrow aperture.

"I'm sorry, Selina, dear," he began in that light, humorous tone that was so much a part of his charm, "but I'm afraid that Dulcie wasn't able to complete her errand." He stepped aside, and I saw a huddled form lying on the floor behind him.

Realization flooded me, and with it came a paralyzing fear.

"It...was...you," I stammered. "It was you who were spying on me, frightening me, trying to make me think I was going insane." I grew sicker with every word. "And now you have added murder to it!"

He raised one heavy eyebrow. "Murder? Oh, Dulcie, you mean. She isn't dead, just unconscious. I couldn't let her bring Marcus and Hiram back here just as you had done me the favor of getting rid of them, could I? But she'll recover in time. And no harm will come to you, either, if you are very cooperative and very quick.''

"What—what do you want?'' I spoke through lips so stiff they could barely form the words.

He smiled again, that infectious smile that lit the brilliant eyes. "Come, now. You know the answer to that. I want Raven's treasure. After you revealed your future plans, I realized I hadn't much time.'' He added in humorous warning, "And don't tell me it isn't in your possession. I read in your face this afternoon that you have found it.''

"No!'' I lied. "You're mistaken, Jared! I don't know—''

The smiling face went suddenly cold. "Don't lie to me! You are very bad at that, Selina.'' The edge left his voice as he stepped nearer and added, "So why don't you facilitate matters and get it for me?''

Though I shrank back in my chair at his approach, my terror was abating enough to allow resentment to kindle into a swift flame of anger. After all, this was not some bestial monster, but only Jared.

"No,'' I said. "I won't. It isn't mine to give.''

With lightning swiftness, he bridged the remaining space between us, and leaning ominously over me, grabbed me by both arms with an iron grip. Slowly, inexorably, he pulled me to my feet. As before, I found myself surprised by the whipcord strength of his slender body. He was not tall, and his mobile face was close to mine as he said with a softness that was more frightening than a loud command, "You *will* give it to me. I have invested six years of my life for this moment. It wouldn't be wise for you to thwart me now.''

I was genuinely surprised at this. "What do you mean?"

He shook me a little, and I bit back a shriek of fright.

"Use your head. Why do you suppose a man of my talents would bury himself in this backwoods town? I was tired of being poor, just as you were. And just as you did, I came here to try to get some of the money that was rightfully mine. If my uncle hadn't died—"

I felt dazed and unable to grasp his meaning. "Your uncle? I don't understand—"

He shook me again. His fingers bit into my flesh so hard I gasped from the pain.

"My uncle was Harry Ingersol, the fourth partner. If he hadn't died so soon after they found the strike, mother would have inherited a great deal. As it was, all she got was his paltry part of the profits the mine had made until his death. His share of the mine reverted to the partners instead of to mother and me, as it should have." His fingers tightened even more. "Now, was that fair? She was his sister. We were entitled to his part of it."

This time I cried aloud, "Please, Jared, you're hurting me!"

He loosened his grip somewhat, but he didn't let me go. "That is nothing to the hurt you will feel if you don't do as I say." His voice softened, and a little amusement crept back into it. "In that instance, I can only hope you are made of sterner stuff than the late Miss Winfield."

As the import of his words struck me, I went cold as ice. I no longer felt the pain from his brutally digging fingers.

"What did you do to her?" I managed to speak casually as though I were only mildly interested in hearing his answer.

"She refused to show me the treasure," he said. His tone implied that she had been quite maddeningly unreasonable. "And I had to have it, now that she had caught me breaking in. You can see that, can't you? But when I—she must have had a weak heart, for I only twisted her arm a little, and—she was gone."

The fury that blazed up in me erased all thought of the danger I was in. "You killed her, then." Rage made my voice unsteady. "That is what it amounts to, isn't it?"

"I didn't want to, Selina," he protested. "Just as I don't want to hurt you. That's why I tried to frighten you away. I really do care for you, you know. But you *would* prefer Marcus—"

I might have done something desperate and foolish in the next moment—tried some escape that would never have worked—but at that instant my eyes were drawn toward Raven's portrait. That steady gaze seemed to hold a note of warning, and I hesitated a fraction of a second. Jared, seeing the direction of my glance, twisted around to follow it. And in that instant I noticed that Dulcie, on the floor of the hidden passageway, was beginning to regain consciousness.

By the time Jared turned back to me, my eyes were steady on his face.

"She wasn't worth it, you know," he said, obviously speaking of Raven. "All that devotion you were prepared to give her. She was a selfish, vindictive woman. Did you discover that she was blackmailing Soames and the others? I deduced it long ago, but I had no way to prove it. Yet with all her money, she wouldn't give me my rightful share." His eyes glittered strangely. "You aren't going to be that way, are you, Selina?"

With iron determination, I kept my eyes from straying to Dulcie.

"No, of course not," I answered. "Why should I be? Marcus is wealthy, and I have enough without the treasure. I was going to give it to charity, anyhow." I attempted to smile. "Would you like to see it?"

His relief was almost childish. "You mean you won't oppose me? Wonderful! I didn't like the thought of hurting you. Tell me where it is and how you found it after I have searched for it all this time."

I was already urging him from the room. "You will just have to curb your curiosity," I said, trying to simulate a mischievous tone. "It is much more exciting to see it than to hear about it." I dared not look back at Dulcie, but I knew that when she regained consciousness, she would immediately seek help, and I needed it most desperately. For in spite of Jared's protestations about hurting me, I realized that even if I gave him the treasure, he wouldn't dare leave me alive after confessing that he had been the cause of Raven's death. My only chance was to escape him in the upper reaches of the mansion, or failing that, delay until Dulcie brought help.

As he followed me to the stairway, I was thinking rapidly. Where should I claim the treasure to be? It was not going to be easy to fool him, not after the many nights he had spent searching. But my instinct told me to lure him to the farthest point in order to delay the longest.

"Just where are we going?" he asked abruptly.

"To the attic. The treasure is in one of the trunks Raven had there."

Suspicion flared in his eyes. "How could it be? I have searched those trunks again and again. How did you find it when I couldn't?"

"Isn't it obvious?" I took a candle and led the way up to the second floor. "There were three of us, and we had all the time in the world and a good light. Grandmother was very clever, but we found it at last."

My skill in lying must have improved miraculously, for he continued to follow me. But at the landing he seized my arm and hurried me up the second flight. "Be quick," he commanded. "Dulcie might possibly revive and seek help. I don't intend to find myself trapped in the attic."

It was at the word "trapped" that a plan sprang full-blown into my mind. Unlike the second floor, the third story had only one staircase. If I could bring my plan about, his words might be a portent of his fate.

The attic door creaked dolefully. "Over there," I said, entering only as far as I thought I must. "The large trunk with the old clothes in it."

To my dismay he grasped my arm and led me to it. Taking the candle from me, he said, "Unearth it, and be quick about it."

Moving as deliberately as I dared, I knelt at the trunk and opened the lid. My heart was pounding in my throat. In only a brief moment he would know the truth, and what might he do then? I had visions of him strangling me and hurling my body into this very trunk, where it wouldn't be found until— The very thought of that "until" made me want to retch. My hands were shaking as I lifted the last of the garments out of the trunk.

"Well?" he demanded. "Where is it?"

I was sending frantic prayers heavenward—whether to God or to Raven, I never knew. "Right here. There is a false bottom, but I can't—"

My prayers were answered. Impatiently, he yanked me aside and pushed the candle into my hand. "Here," he said eagerly, "let me," and he leaned over to peer into the trunk.

I seized my chance. Dropping the candle, which plunged the attic into darkness, I rammed against him with all my strength. He went headfirst into the empty trunk, and I groped for the lid and slammed it down upon him. It must have caught him heavily across the back, for he yelled with pain. I remember hoping that I had broken his spine. With whirlwind speed I ran to the door, wrenched it open and stumbled into the blackness of the hall. As we had come up, I had noted a heavy carved chair just outside the attic, and I fumbled for it and quickly shoved it under the doorknob before running to the stairway. Terror lent wings to my feet, and it seemed that I barely touched the treads as I flew down the two flights of stairs.

I leaped down the last few steps and ran toward freedom, only to see Jared emerging from the library door to intercept me.

I was so stunned that I couldn't even try to get away. I could only cling to the arm that barred my way while despair drained the last of my strength from me. "How—did you do it?"

"Raven left nothing to chance," he said. "I'll have to give her that. The secret passageway goes all the way to the attic." He came closer. "But the time for tricks is over, Selina. Dulcie is gone, which means someone will be here any moment. Get me the treasure or I'll have to kill you."

He would kill me in any case. Dully, I said, "It isn't worth my life. It's in the library, behind a secret panel of the wall."

Viciously, he yanked me to him. "You had better not be lying." A deep gash over one eye oozed blood at each throb of his temple.

"I'm not lying. There is a secret panel in the wall."

He pushed me before him into the library. I was too spent to resist. At his command, I stumbled to the cupboard containing Raven's appointment books and knelt before it. It was absurd to carry the deception this far, but it was as though we were players in a farce that had to be acted out until the very end. I took out the books and pulled the nail to let the panel slide down. "In there," I said tonelessly.

He eyed it warily. "What could be hidden in there?"

"Gold dust," I improvised. "Sacks of it. Take them and go away."

I hoped that in his excitement he would let go of me and kneel to get it himself, but he was not that foolish again. Holding me firmly with one hand, he reached to feel the niche's interior with the other. After a moment of futile groping, he turned to look at me, and I could see my own death in his eyes.

He rose, pulling me with him, and for a moment we stood together in some sort of macabre embrace. Then, slowly and with evident enjoyment, he twisted my arm behind my back.

"You never intended to give it to me, did you?" The blue eyes were smiling vilely into mine.

"No! Not if you killed me!" Then I screamed in agony as he shoved my arm so high I thought it had broken. The pain was unbelievable, and I shrieked again and felt myself sliding into a faint.

But before the darkness closely entirely over me, the pressure eased, and I fell to the floor, sobbing uncontrollably. I was dimly aware of a struggle going on above me, of thuds and grunts and furniture smashing. Then there was only the sound of heavy breathing, and Marcus was kneeling beside me, cradling me in his arms.

"Oh, my darling girl, where has he hurt you?" I heard him say.

"My arm," I answered, sobbing. "I thought he would break it."

"Dulcie," Marcus snapped. "Go get Doc Gentry." I felt him scoop me up and lay me down on the sofa. "It had better not be broken," he said, his voice strangely thick, "or our Mr. Newcomb won't be writing a word for a long time to come."

I looked beyond Marcus. Hiram was holding Jared in a grip very mindful of the way the editor had grasped me, and from his expression Jared was finding it no more pleasant than I had. He looked a wreck. In addition to the cut over his eye that I had inflicted, one side of his face was puffing out enormously, and his nose was dripping blood and pointing off at a strange angle. Yet he managed to give me that funny, twisted grin.

"No hard feelings, I hope, Selina. After all, I had to give it my best."

Despite Marcus's protestations, I struggled to a sitting position. "*No hard feelings*? You meant to murder me!"

He shrugged. "Are you sure of that? I only twisted your arm a little. Perhaps the rest was only talk."

"And my grandmother? You twisted her arm a little, and she died. Are there to be no hard feelings about that, either?"

The blue eyes were innocent. "Miss Winfield? The *Bulletin* said she died of heart failure."

Enraged, Hiram yanked Jared into a painful position. "Dast I hurt him some, Miss Selina?" He looked as though he longed to do it.

"Better not, Hiram," Marcus said reluctantly. "We'll have to let the law take care of him. Put him down. I want to ask him a few questions."

Again the crooked grin, ludicrous beside the swelling jaw. "Anything to be obliging, Marcus."

"That night we searched the attic. You got out through the passageway?"

"Of course. I found it helpful on several occasions."

"I've been standing guard around the mansion on nights when you have gotten in. How did you get past me?"

Jared hesitated, then shrugged. "I suppose I may as well tell you, since you can follow the passageway and learn for yourself. A tunnel leads in from the well house at the back of the property, well beyond the perimeter where you stood guard." He grinned at me. "You nearly fooled me once, my dear, when you pretended to be overcome by weariness. I was so startled I foolishly bolted from the tunnel, then had to call on you as an excuse for being in the vicinity. I'm sure you will forgive the lateness of the hour."

At the memories his words invoked, I shuddered involuntarily. "How did you know about the secret passageway?" I demanded. "You are apparently the only one who did know, except Raven."

In spite of the crooked nose and the blood trickling from the gash on his head, Jared managed to assume a jaunty look. "My dear, it is my business to learn things no one else knows. The man who built the place, rest his soul, was susceptible to flattery. If Raven had been wise, she would have had him destroyed after he had completed it, just as the Egyptian kings did with their tomb builders."

"I've heard enough." Marcus looked revulsed. "Hiram, let's take him on down to the sheriff."

"Wait," I protested. At that moment, I knew all too well how Raven must have felt. "Just to convince

Jared there are no hard feelings, I want to show him something. Hiram, bring him into the parlor."

Hiram dragged Jared to his feet. The editor had an odd look on his face. "Selina—is it the treasure? You really did find it?"

Without answering, I got up and crossed the hall to the parlor. Standing beneath Raven's portrait, I turned to face Jared. Hiram and Marcus stood just behind.

"You have no doubt been within reach of it many times, Jared, *my friend*." I didn't try to keep the note of sarcastic satisfaction from my voice. "If you will move a few steps closer, you will be within reach of it again."

Like a man in a daze, he freed himself from Hiram's loosening grip and came closer. "Where?" he asked, looking around. "I don't see—"

And then, all at once, he did see, just as I had. His eyes had fallen on the matching crystal beads that hung all around the overtrimmed silk shade of a nearby lamp, and he saw that they shone with an unusual brilliance and that, instead of a hole being drilled to suspend them, each had been hung in a delicate wire casing. I guessed them to be at least three carats apiece, and there were seventeen of them, one for every year that my grandmother had lived in Raven's Rise.

"Do you mean that they have been hanging here all this time?" His eyes were sick. "And that I have sat within—" He choked at the thought and couldn't go on.

"There are other things, of course," I said smugly. "For instance, the frame of the miniature on the table is solid gold, as you would discover if you picked it up. The figurines on the mantelpiece—they were hollow and have been filled with gold. In fact, nearly everything in this room has some enrichment that puts it far beyond its original value. I would be happy to point the rest of them out to you, if you wish. It will give you something to remember all those long, dark nights in prison.''

Jared tore his eyes away from the diamond-trimmed lamp and looked at me. He even managed a semblance of his crooked smile. ''Be careful, Selina,'' he cautioned me lightly. ''It seems there is more of your grandmother in you than you might like to believe.''

Hiram took him away then, and Marcus went, too, to make doubly sure that he would be put safely behind bars. I sat alone in the parlor, waiting for Dr. Gentry.

That was a part of what you wanted, wasn't it, grandmother? You wanted him brought to justice. Well, it will be done, and I, too, am glad. But I wish I could feel about you as I did at first. Perhaps if you had had a better reason—

My reverie was interrupted by Dr. Gentry.

''Here you are,'' he said as he stuck his head in the door. ''Dulcie said your arm might be broken. I sent her on to bed, by the way. Got a lump on her head big as a duck egg.''

''But is she all right?'' I asked anxiously. I started to rise.

''Just stay right there. Hiram'll be here soon to take care of her. You let me take a look at that arm.''

''It's not broken, just extremely sore.''

A moment's examination confirmed my diagnosis, and he sat rather heavily in the chair across from me. I seized my opportunity.

"Dr. Gentry, I know a great deal about my grandmother now. Will you answer one or two last questions?"

The kindly eyes looked into mine. "I suppose I could do that. Depending on what they are."

"It was you, wasn't it, who caused my ring to be returned."

Dr. Gentry hesitated. "I may have dropped a hint or two to Soames."

"Did you send me the two hundred dollars?"

He sighed. I could read the answer in his face.

"Then you knew all along that I was alive, knew where I was. Why didn't you ever tell Raven about me?"

He sighed again, and the lines in his face deepened. "I guess I didn't want to play God, Selina. A doctor has to do that a lot, you know. In your case, you were well fed, decently cared for—after all, Henry was your father. And Raven—well, much as I loved her, I couldn't see that she would make you happy here. This obsession she had left her no room for anything else."

I wondered how much he knew. "You mean, her need for revenge over Will's death?"

The bushy eyebrows raised. "No, not that, though that was bad enough. It was her obsession with Bittercreek—everything she did was because of that. She wanted it as a monument for Will. She got it in her head that as long as Bittercreek existed, he lived, too, and she spent the rest of her life trying to keep things together." He shot a glance at me. "The—the things she did to Soames and Ogilvey—that was why. She knew that if the richest men in town pulled out, so would everyone else, and Bittercreek would be just a memory."

"What about you, Dr. Gentry," I asked softly. "How did she get you to stay all these years? Did she have to blackmail you into it, too?"

Sudden pain knit the heavy brows together. It was a moment before he answered me.

"So you figured that out, too, did you? If I had known you were so smart, I might've left you in San Francisco." He was silent for a moment, then went on. "No, Raven never knew what really happened about the note." He looked down at his hands. "I got it, all right, but I didn't go to Will. Afterward, I wasn't sure why. Maybe it was fear—I never was the bravest man in the world—maybe jealousy. I knew I didn't stand a chance with Raven as long as Will was around. But it was no sooner done than I regretted it—and I've spent the rest of my life trying to atone for it. I did exactly what Raven wanted me to do. I stayed in this town, and I stayed her friend. And I never tried to be anything else, though there was a time—" He stopped speaking and rubbed his face in a familiar gesture. "Doesn't really matter anymore. Raven's gone, and soon the town will be gone. And I don't suppose the world will be any worse for it."

After a while Dr. Gentry took his leave, but not before giving me orders about my arm.

Later, when Marcus came in and took me into his embrace, I hardly noticed any pain at all. "I love you so, my darling," he murmured against my hair. "Everything I did was because of that. I was so afraid I might lose you."

"You won't lose me, Marcus—ever," I whispered. "We'll be the happiest couple in San Francisco."

He held me away from him. "You mean you'll go? What about Raven's Rise?"

"I planned it all while waiting for you," I said. "Next week, at the ball, I'll announce that I'm going to turn it into an orphanage. I'll put Mrs. Henderson and Ellie in charge of it, and the money from the treasure will keep it going." I got caught up in the excitement of my own vision. "Oh, Marcus, imagine how wonderful it will be to have children laughing and playing and running in and out of all these empty rooms! Don't you think grandmother would be pleased?"

He smiled indulgently. "And just where are you going to get all these orphans?"

"There are lots of them in San Francisco, most of them worse off than I was. Bittercreek will be a good place for them to grow up in, and if it survives, perhaps some of them will settle here. And it will survive," I added fiercely, "if I have to do a little blackmailing myself!"

"Spoken like a true mistress of Raven's Rise," he said. And then he took me in his arms again, and we forgot that the mansion even existed.

·Harlequin·

Harlequin Romance

The Winds of Winter
Sandra Field

Tender, captivating stories
that sweep to faraway
places and delight with the
magic of love.

Harlequin Presents...

VIOLET WINSPEAR

time of the temptress

Exciting romance novels
for the woman of today—
rare blend of passion and
dramatic realism.

Sensual and romantic
stories about choices,
dilemmas, resolutions, a
above all, the fulfillment
of love.

Harlequin Temptation

First Impressions
MARIS SOULE

GEN-A-2

Harlequin is romance...

INDULGE IN THE PLEASURE OF SUPERB ROMANCE READING BY CHOOSING THE MOST POPULAR LOVE STORIES IN THE WORLD

Longer, more absorbing love stories for the connoisseur of romantic fiction.

An innovative series blending contemporary romance with fast-paced adventure.

Contemporary romances— uniquely North American in flavor and appeal.

and you can never have too much romance.